A Fine Racy Wine

by

Kate Fitzroy

Prologue

This was not the right time to be fashionably late, but the London traffic had congealed into a solid angry mass in Sloane Square. The taxi driver glanced happily at his ticking meter. and then at me in his rear-view mirror.

'Nothing I can do, miss.' Then, after a small pause, 'I know you, don't I? You're that posh totty on the TV, going on about wine. You're Eve Sinclair, aren't you?'

I flashed my professional smile which lasted at least a microsecond and nodded, then looked out of the side window. People were hurrying by; the usual nine o'clock morning crush and rush of London workers, heads lowered against the driving rain. The scene was full of anxious people late for work, wanting to get out of the rain and begin their week. I sighed and envied them their silent anonymity. Did any of them wish they could have my place in the transient fame of the media world? The taxi inched forward and then drew to a halt as the traffic lights turned red again.

'Not going nowhere fast this morning. Bet you wish you was in one of those vineyards in France or Italy. Blimey, what a golden life you lead.'

His words stung me into consciousness. Over the last few months, I had become horribly aware that I was a very spoilt and lucky young woman. I had always been a spoiled child, but then, when my father suddenly lost his millions and fell into the disgrace shared by many city bankers, I had been stunned into action. True, I had at first sulked and even cried hot tears of self-pity, but reality eventually hit below my Versace belt when my Coutts Silk charge card seemed to have become inflexible. At twenty-seven I had begun to earn my living for the first time. Until then, after an illustrious and extended academic time, I had left Cambridge, turning down the fellowship I was offered, and gone to live in the *Provençal mas*, given to me as a twenty-first birthday present from my father. So, when the financial crash banged loud and clear into my perfect life, I was to be found writing obscure poetry, sitting under my favourite olive tree beside my turquoise swimming pool.

That was what I would call a golden life. Now, I cleared a patch in the steamy window of the cab and looked at the stagnant traffic. My life may have been idle and luxurious, but I had an inherent dislike of being late. Maybe I could blame my father for that as well as a million other things.

'Sorry, I'll have to run for it.' I hastily pushed a ten-pound note through to the cab driver and jumped out of the taxi. True, my black patent loafers landed into a puddle, but anything was better than being trapped into a conversation that would inevitably lead to my infamous father and his disappearance. I was very weary of trying to make excuses for his sudden escape. Anyway, what could I say that would please anyone? All I knew was that he was alive and well and living in some remote coastal village in the Arabian Sea. I received a postcard at the beginning of every month to tell me just that, and nothing more. No return address offered and, frankly, I'm not at all sure I would have replied to him anyway. He had chosen to desert me, just like my mother had many years earlier. Well, not quite the same, I had to admit. She had run off when I was only five years old, demanding a divorce from my father and forgetting my existence. Did I blame her, bear a long term grudge? I looked up at the grey London sky above me and almost smiled. She would have made a disastrous mother, and was truly much better off with her third, or maybe now fourth husband in sunny California. But my father... my thoughts were interrupted by my mobile ringing. I ducked into the cover of Peter Jones doorway and answered it. Now I really was smiling as I saw the call was from Adam.

'Hello, Adam... are you in London yet?'

'Good morning, Princess. Yes, I am back in good old Blighty, enjoying the rain. This absolutely isn't Pompeii though, is it? You promised me our next assignment was Pompeii... I have been dreaming about Sorrento and the bright light on the blue slices of the Med. How could you do this to me?'

'Sorry, Adam. I know it's rather rotten…'

'Rather rotten. Oh, my dear Princess, I had quite forgotten your archaic English. It's not rather rotten it's effing awful.'

'Well, I suppose so, but it's not my fault. My publishers had the bright idea to have an English vineyard story for chapter six. I'm on my way there now to get all the details. I think they want me to write up about a vineyard in Suffolk.'

'Suffolk? Can they actually grow grapes in Suffolk?'

'Well, yes, I'm sure it will be German stock vines, you know, maybe the grape varieties Angevine, Bacchus…'

'OK, OK, I believe you. Spare me the lecture. I shall never understand how you can make wine sound so much sexier on your TV programmes. Anyway, buzz me when you know where and when we can meet up. Bernard is on his way up from Dover right now, so we'll soon be together again.'

'Fine. Give me an hour or so, and I'll get back to you.' I rang off and felt a decided jolt in my stomach as I lost contact. I looked out at the rainswept pavement and wondered why and how Adam Wright could have this effect on me. We had been working together for nearly six months now, and he was certainly a most talented photographer, enjoying a meteoric rise to fame in London after the exhibition of his war photos from Afghanistan. I quite understood that this assignment, working with me in the quiet and gentle vineyards of Italy and France, had been therapeutic for him. Did he realise that it was much the same for me? I was still in recovery from the drastic change in my lifestyle. The taxi driver was half right, I did lead a golden life. But everything is relative and if I had managed to claw my way back, using wealthy contacts, pulling the right strings to open the doors to my new life in the media, well, it was still an enormous effort. I had been so accustomed to everything falling into my lap, that it was very hard to be obsequious and grateful for the crumbs that were thrown to me. Fortunately, while up at Cambridge, I had side-stepped and taken a Master of Wine course. Strangely enough, it was that piece of paper that now ran my life, and not my useless master's degree in literature. Ironic? Maybe, but use it I did. I had soon found that everyone enjoys a riches to rags story. Part of my media fame depended on the curiosity of the public, the desire to see how some poor little rich girl was going to cope with working for her living.

I stepped out into the driving rain, squared my shoulders and pushed my chin up. I would show them, I would show them all.

'I have just about forgiven you for not taking me to Pompeii now, Princess. And I have to say that you have found a fun part of Suffolk.'

Adam was sitting beside me in the back of the Mercedes limousine and Bernard was at the wheel, driving us fast toward Newmarket. We had all met up in London and now we were on the last stretch of our journey. The road was as straight as an arrow and flanked on both sides by immaculate grassy paddocks. The rain had almost given up on the day, and there was a pale shimmer of sunlight between the tall trees. Adam was leaning his head back against the leather headrest, totally relaxed. There was something about being with him that made it almost impossible to worry about anything. That, and the familiar and comforting sight of the back of Bernard's solid neck, made me sigh with contentment. Maybe I was wrong, perhaps it was just being back with Bernard that made me feel so secure? He had been the sole constant in my life for as long as I could remember. Wherever I went, Bernard had taken me. Although he had initially been my father's driver for work, it was soon established that he would drive me. My father trusted him implicitly, and I think, in many ways, he was my father's best friend. Certainly, when the financial crash ripped our lives apart, Bernard remained loyal and determined to stay with me as much as possible. As soon as I had landed my media work, I had insisted that Bernard was crafted into my contract. If the TV channel or my publishers wanted me to go anywhere, I made sure it would be with Bernard driving me. In fact, it was only when they readily agreed to this clause that I began to realise I was a valuable asset. I sighed again and Adam turned to me.

'Did you hear that, Bernie? The Princess gave one of her sighs. Now, was it a happy sort of kitten purr or was it one of her waspish out of humour sighs? What do you think, Bernie.'

'I am sorry, Adam, but I did not hear.'

Adam slapped his hand on his denim-clad knee, 'You're an old devil, Bernie. You heard perfectly well. That was just one of your smart-alec answers.'

'Smart Alec? Who is this?'

'Oh please!' I put my hands over my ears, 'Please don't start on the idiom thing. We haven't even arrived yet.'

Adam sat up straight, 'Well, I'm ashamed of you, Princess Clever Clogs, and you a Cambridge don. You know that you should be only too glad to enrich Bernard's impoverished English.'

'I don't think the term Smart Alec is particularly enhancing, and Bernard speaks very good English and a lot better than your French.'

'That's all very well, but Bernard is anxious to improve his English. He wants to impress his girlfriend.'

I saw Bernard glance into the driving mirror and frown at Adam as he said, 'Is true, I want to improve my English, but be careful, young man, remember the ducking in the fountain at Frascati? Elaine is my teacher and not my girlfriend. You must be polite when you speak of her.'

'Not your girlfriend. Crikey, Bernie, you've just spent two weeks holiday at her place in Roussillon, don't tell me…'

I interrupted, as I often did, by changing the subject. 'Look at that statue on the roundabout. It's really rather good and definitely lets you know you're about to enter the racing town of Newmarket.'

'Yeah, it is good. Must be a famous horse, I guess. Look, race course on either side now and right royal hedges. A golf club, of course… or rather along the race course. Look, another statue… is that our little Queen with some horses? So, here we are then, Royal Newmarket. Looks like a fun town to me.'

We were now driving slowly along the crowded High Street, and it did have a different air to the usual country market town. There was a string of black and yellow taxis along one side of the road that would not have looked out of place in New York. Opposite stood an imposing red brick building called the Jockey Club, then a Racing Museum and more betting shops, clubs and nail bars than the usual building societies and charity shops. There was a definite buzz and flurry to the place. We circled a Victorian clock tower, and drew away from the centre between green stretches of gallops and large houses with stabling. Bernard glanced at the satnav and said,

'The hotel is now three miles the other side of the town. Do you want to stop for anything?'

'No, let's just get there now.' I answered too snappily and then hastily turned to Adam, 'Unless you want to stop, Adam?'

I always did this. I just didn't think quickly enough. I was so accustomed to giving orders and pleasing myself, that it had been a slow learning process to think that there was anyone else in the car. I certainly didn't intend to be rude, but very often it caused a row between Adam and me. In fact, we argued quite a lot, but our bad humour never lasted long. Now, he just smiled at me. He did have the most engaging, slightly crooked smile.

'Don't worry, your Royal Highness. I don't want to stop either, but thank you for condescending to ask me.'

I looked away from him, trying not to show that I was now rather angry. He would insist on calling me Princess or your Royal Highness, just to show me how haughty he thought I could be. It was infuriating, especially when I was trying my very best to be so civil.

I leant forward, ignoring Adam and spoke to Bernard as I looked at the small satnav screen. 'Do you know the Royal Park Hotel, Bernard?'

'*Mais oui*, Mademoiselle Eve. I have drived your father here two or three times in the past. As you know, he did not like the racing, but often he was invited to the business occasions. Always, when we drove back to London, he would be laughing. I remember once he told me it was called the Sport of Kings, but he thought it more like animated roulette. Then he tried a joke on me.'

I looked at Bernard in surprise. He seemed to know a side of my father that I had never seen. Certainly, my father had always been gentle and humorous enough, ever ready to educate me on some point, but I had never known him tell a joke.

'A joke? Do you remember it?'

'*Mais oui!* Your father, he say in a very serious voice, Bernard, do you know how to make a small fortune betting on race horses?'

I sat back in the car and thought about it and then I looked at Adam. 'Do you know the joke, Adam?'

'No, go on, Bernie, tell us! How do you make a small fortune betting on race horses?'

Bernard gave a chuckle as though he remembered the very moment,

'You have to start with a large fortune.'

So, it was with good humour restored in the car that we arrived at the Royal Park Hotel. I had booked the hotel for a week, the time that I always hoped it would take to write one of my chapters, although often we fell into some difficulty or other… not always related to wine. My expense account was very heavy, but so far my publishers had not grumbled aloud. My TV series had soared to a top rating by some miracle. I had no idea why or how, but I exploited the success for all it was worth, knowing that it could be ephemeral. It was a world that I had no understanding of at all and even less respect. My media agent, Melanie, arranged everything and coerced me into accepting all invitations to attend prestigious wine-tasting functions, and, even worse, appear on brainless chat and quiz shows. I quite understood that my success partly depended on her efforts, and I was grudgingly grateful. I would fall into a moody bad humour before any event, but luckily, when adrenalin kicked in, I found I could perform like a clever monkey. I had just read a review on my latest quiz show performance and was amused to learn that, apparently, I had shown my usual 'acerbic wit.'

Now, still smiling at my father's simple joke, I decided that acerbic didn't really fit my sense of humour at all. I was pleased to be back in the tolerant and comfortable company of Bernard… and Adam, too. I glanced sideways at Adam and saw he already had his camera in one hand and the other on the car door handle ready to jump out the moment the car stopped. I felt a rush of affection for him and his enthusiasm for everything that life threw his way. Affection… or was it more? Before I could ponder on that, fortunately, the car stopped, and my door was opened by a tall man in a well-cut grey lounge suit.

'Miss Sinclair, welcome to the Royal Park. My name is David West, I'm the concierge here and delighted to greet you.'

'Good evening, it's good to be here.' I stepped out of the car and looked at this David West. Had he known my father? Was he about to launch into some mention of him that I would have to field? The people that had known my father, a large number of people, fell into two distinct camps. Many were still very angry at his precipitous fall from his high tower of power in the City of London. On the other side, almost as many seemed to hold him in respect and even great affection. I had no need to worry. David West smiled down at me, the perfect image of a diplomatic and welcoming host.

'Did you have a good journey?'

And so, my fears of an awkward moment passed quickly, and I went into the foyer, relieved and relaxed again.

The receptionist, almost obscured behind a huge vase of orchids, smiled at me coldly,

'Good Evening, Miss Sinclair, welcome to the Royal Park Hotel, will you sign the register please.'

I took up the pen she offered and signed us in, thinking how it was one thing to be professional and quite another to be genuinely welcoming. The young woman swivelled the leather-bound register around the moment I had signed and continued in a rather bored voice.

'Your rooms are ready. I see you have reserved three rooms… one suite and two single rooms, is that correct?'

I realised she was looking curiously at Adam who was leaning with his back against the reception desk, his long blonde hair shining in the light of the overhead chandelier. He was wearing his old Parka, as usual, but he had a natural confidence that could take him anywhere. Was this young woman wondering why I wasn't sharing my suite with him? Had the same question often popped into my own head? I looked at her severely,

'Quite correct, thank you. I'm rather tired so please show us to our rooms quickly. Oh, and I should like to book a massage in the spa… as soon as possible.'

The young woman looked flustered and began to open another leather-bound book on her desk. The charming David West loomed into sight,

'No problem, Miss Sinclair.' He leant toward the receptionist and spoke to her through the sprigs of white orchids, 'Miss Sinclair is our VVIP guest, and we must look after her very well.' He smiled, but there was a steely look in his eye as he gave his discreet warning. Then he turned back to me again, 'I'll pop across to the Spa now and make sure they are ready for you. We have an excellent masseuse here. Please take my card and just call me if there is absolutely anything more that I can arrange for you.'

I smiled at David West, appreciating that he was definitely the guy who knew how to manage the arrival of a tired guest.

'Why thank you, David, if I may call you that, and please call me Eve. That would be great, and I'll have a quick swim before dinner. Could you book a table for three about 8 o'clock?'

'Absolutely, eight pm. We have three restaurants… Italian, French Bistro or Cordon Bleu…' He hesitated and then, so did I. Damn, I had done it again. I turned quickly to Adam and Bernard,

'Sorry, would either of you like to swim or have a massage? What about you, Bernard, would you like a massage after your long drive up from France?'

'*Mais non*, Mademoiselle Eve. I shall be happy to go to my room and take a hot shower and a little rest before we eat.'

Adam turned to me and then glanced at the receptionist, giving her the full benefit of his lop-sided and wicked smile and a piercing look from his cornflower blue eyes. Was he actually flirting with the receptionist? Or was he, in some vague way, sharing a joke at my expense as he said,

'No need to think about asking me, Princess. I hate the whole idea of all that Spa nonsense. I shall have a stroll around with my camera before the last light fades from these changeable Suffolk skies. But Italian dinner sounds good.'

I took in a quick breath and then replied as casually as I could,

'Oh, I was thinking about the French Bistro?'

Adam laughed and pulled his camera out of his Parka pocket and strolled off, calling back over his shoulder, 'French Bistro it is then, see you both there at eight.'

There it was again, that sudden flash of anger inside me that Adam often provoked. I watched him stride through the glass entrance doors, his broad angular shoulders outlined against the pale grey light of early evening. Why did he have to be so prickly... and why did I?

We were sitting at a large round table laid for three in the Royal Park Hotel's Italian restaurant. With a quick phone call to the obliging David West, I had out-manoeuvred Adam and changed our booking from the French Bistro to a table at the hotel's Trattoria. The last thing I wanted was to give him any excuse to sulk. There again, he never did sulk, having a naturally sunny and forgiving nature. I was ashamed to admit to myself that I had actually thought to choose Italian and had only gone for the French bistro in some childish and petulant mood. But no, I would not admit it, even to myself.

As the large oval dishes of antipasto arrived at our table, I was pleased to find that Adam was in splendid and celebratory mood. He had obviously just showered, and his hair was shining a damp gold in the candlelight. Bernard, too, looked rested and very handsome in his dark Gallic way, immaculately dressed in a navy suit and crisp white collar. I sighed with satisfaction.

'Now, you can't have missed that Royal sigh, Bernie. I would say it was a small Princessy sigh of self-satisfaction. What do you think?'

'I think is time to eat. Mademoiselle Eve, may I pass you some bread?'

'Ever the social diplomat, Bernie, you're the man. God, I'm so hungry, just look at that prosciutto. Let me at it, my sweet Princess, after you have delicately taken a small slice to nibble, of course.'

I helped myself to more meat than I would normally take and passed the plate to Adam. I found myself annoyed and surprised that the small personal pronoun, 'my', in front of the word 'Princess' had made me blush with delight. Just when I had decided to tell him off for continuing to call me by that ridiculous title. I decided to tackle Bernard instead.

'You know, Bernard, you promised some time ago to drop the Mademoiselle word. Have you forgotten over the last two weeks holiday?'

'Sorry, Eve, but you know I find it very difficult to change after all these years.'

'Did you call Eve, Mademoiselle, even when she was a little girl?' Adam asked, his dark, blonde eyebrows raised in surprised arches.

'*Bien sur, always, mais oui, mais oui.* But I try very hard now to remember to say Eve.'

'Didn't you think it strange that a man old enough to be your father called you Mademoiselle?' Adam turned to me, his blue eyes shining with amusement.

I thought about it for a moment and decided it was once more time for a change of subject.

'A funny or strange thing happened when I was on my way to the Spa.'

Adam laughed aloud, 'That sounds like the beginning of a bad joke, Princess.'

I looked at him in puzzlement, but Bernard spoke before I could ask Adam what he meant.

'*Oh là là*, Eve, please be careful. Remember when you find something funny-strange it always ends in trouble.'

Now, I looked at them both and shook my head, 'No, it was probably nothing. You're quite right, I should just forget about it.' I picked up my knife and fork and studied the food on my plate... and waited.

There was a brief silence and then Adam spoke, 'Okay, you win. Tell us about your funny-strange thing.'

'No, no, I'm sure it was nothing.' I speared a large, black olive and twisted my fork around as though I was examining it. 'Nothing, really.'

Bernard sighed, 'Now you must tell us... is too late to say nothing.'

I looked up at them both innocently, stretching my eyes wide. 'Well, if you really want to know then...'

'Don't bat your long spiky, spidery eyelashes at me like that, Princess... and please don't tell me that you heard a woman crying...' Adam was interrupted by Bernard.

'No indeed, this happened before and made us very much trouble... remember in Provence and then... in Tuscany. No, a woman crying, *mais non, pas encore*.'

'You are both being quite ridiculous.' I was going to challenge Adam's odd description of my eyelashes but decided against it as it could so easily lead to one of our illogical arguments, 'Of course, it wasn't a woman crying... in fact, it was a man shouting very loud indeed.'

'Hmm, well, is that so very strange?'Adam leant toward me and spoke quietly, 'I mean, take a look at the other tables. There's quite a rich mix of lively characters, I'd say. Not exactly sleepy Suffolk, is it?'

'True, and of course, with the races on this week, there must be quite a lot of tension around but... well, this man was shouting and then suddenly stopped, and I heard a crash as though he had fallen or been pushed over.'

'OK, so it was probably a bit of scuffle. Probably over money. But none of your business, Princess. Let's leave it at that.'

'*D'accord*, I agree totally.' Bernard nodded and frowned at me, 'Is nothing to do with you, Eve.'

I shrugged, 'Well, I quite see your point, but the thing is, that's not quite right. You see, they mentioned my name. The man that was shouting said quite clearly that it was bloody difficult now that Eve Sinclair had turned up at the Royal Park Hotel. His language, not mine, of course.'

Adam and Bernard both stopped eating, put down their knives and forks and stared at me. I carried on eating and let the silence that followed my words spread across the table.

We had spent the rest of the meal, a very good meal, debating why anyone should mention my name in the middle of an argument. By the time the Tiramisu had arrived, we were all frustrated and tired of the subject. We had surreptitiously looked at each table in the restaurant, trying to find any likely owners of the angry voices without success. Then, when the coffee arrived a young man came up to our table and asked for an autograph. I had reached for my handbag to find my pen, before I realised he was asking Adam for his autograph, not me. Adam chatted with the young man for quite a while about making a career in photo-journalism. I was interested to see that he showed the young man his small black moleskin notebook, advising him to keep written records. I had often wondered just what it was that Adam scribbled down at odd moments on our travels. I tried to peep at the open page but could only make out some figures jotted down in rows, and now he had moved on to talk about technical details. I caught Bernard's eye and he nodded to me and we decided to leave Adam to his conversation. Bernard accompanied me to the door of my suite, and I pointed out the door of the room where the men had been shouting. Now, it was closed and the whole corridor silent and peaceful. I even wondered if I had heard correctly and said so to Bernard as we parted. It had been a long day for both of us.

So, it wasn't until we were in the car the next day that I suddenly announced,

'Oh my goodness. I've just realised something. One of the angry voices had a strong Irish accent.'

Adam, who had been sitting beside me in the back of the car, quieter than usual, turned to me abruptly.

'Irish? Holy moly, Eve. I thought all yesterday evening you said you couldn't remember a thing more.'

'Yes, sorry about that. Honestly, it's just come to me. I was thinking the brief moment over yet again and, just in my head, I heard the words and the accent. Definitely Irish.'

'I wish you had thought of it last night. I spent hours in the bar, after you and Bernard deserted me. I tried to get into several conversations, thinking I might find a clue to why your appearance at the Royal Park should so annoy anyone. If I had known I could listen out for an Irish accent.. well, really Eve… it's so maddening to say that only now you remember.'

Bernard interrupted, '*Non, non*, Adam, is not the fault of Eve. Is very normal. Many times when I was taking the statements, when I was in the police, yes, many times small details are remembered after by a witness, sometimes days after the event.'

I looked at Bernard with gratitude. I realised it was exasperating that I had only just recalled the voice more accurately, but that's just how it was. I turned to Adam,

'I've said I'm sorry, but I had no idea you stayed up late trying to find out more. I don't suppose it was so much of a hardship to hang out in the bar, anyway.'

'You know quite well that I only drink water, Eve but, OK, truth is I did have quite a good time. There was a group of girls from Chelmsford out for a laugh. Getting paralytic but very amusing.'

'Really? Sounds such fun.' I turned away from him and looked out the car window at the gentle Suffolk countryside rolling past. I knew I had no claims of any sort on Adam's private life, but I felt horribly jealous. Essex girls on the lookout for fun could eat Adam alive. He was ridiculously unaware of his Jesus-like good looks, or so it seemed to me. But what did I really know?

'As you don't drink alcohol I would have thought it rather boring being a witness to anyone getting drunk.'

'Absolutely, you're quite right, Princess Goody-Two-Shoes. Anyway, I soon peeled myself away from the girls, and I got talking with a very interesting young guy. A farrier.'

'A farrier?' I looked at him in surprise.

'I know, who ever gets to be a farrier? At first I though he was a harrier. I mean, I've heard about cross-country running... harriers and all that. I had a friend who was in the Victoria Park Harriers but anyway, this lad's a farrier.'

'A farrier, well, of course, here in Newmarket there must be lots of work for them.'

Adam leant forward in the car and spoke to Bernard who had been listening to our conversation, as he drove through the narrow country lanes.

'Another chance to improve your vocab, Bernie. F is for farrier, the guy who give horses a hooficure.'

'Hooficure? Sorry, Adam, but this I don't understand.'

'For goodness sakes, Adam, what are you on about? Bernard, Adam is trying to explain that a farrier is a man who cares for the hooves of horses and fits them with shoes. It must be an extremely important job in a racing stable.'

'Ah, I understand, *il est maréchal-ferrant, un forgeron.* Yes, there must be good work here in all the big stables.'

'Well, now that's sorted, I'll tell you more.' Adam nodded and continued, 'He's working all hours and saving up to be married... and guess what, his fiancée was the girl that gave you your massage, Princess.'

'Really? How do you know?'

'Well, when she finished work she had gone back to their place... they have a flat over the stables where he works... and told him that she had just massaged the famous celeb, Eve Sinclair.'

'Not very discreet of her.'

'Oh, don't be stuffy, Princess, we were just chatting, and he said that Lois though you were very beautiful.'

'Hmm, I suppose that's meant to make me feel better about idle chatter. Is she called Lois then?'

'Well, yes, I'd have thought you'd have know that after spending over an hour with her.'

'Gracious, no. I never talk to anyone unless I have to.'

Adam laughed aloud, 'You are a priceless Princess, do you know that? Anyway, enough idle chatter. We seem to have arrived at your appointed vineyard.'

Bernard swung the heavy Mercedes to a halt in front of a pair of impressive heavy oak gates and waited as they swung open automatically. We continued up a long driveway lined with leafy lime trees toward a splendid Tudor manor house. It was everything an important mediaeval country house should be. It nestled into the surrounding green Suffolk fields and oak forests, exuding a history of comfortable wealth. The half-timbered and pargetted walls glowed golden ochre in the dull light, and six red brick chimneys twisted high above the pan-tiled roof into the white-grey sky. I sat forward in my seat, keen to take in the detail of my first impression. Yes, it was even better than the photos I had already examined on their website. In fact, the photos did not do it justice at all. I felt a ripple of excited satisfaction as I thought that this Suffolk gem would do very nicely for Chapter Six of my book. I grabbed my tote bag and looked forward to starting work, forgetting all about angry voices, Irish or otherwise.

'This is definitely not the sunny Italian Pompeii trip you promised me, Princess.' Adam was trudging along beside me between the rain-soaked vines. The pouring rain easily penetrated the canopy of leaves arched across the arboured structure of the vineyard.

'Do you have to keep going on about Pompeii? It's not my fault. The publishers decided that the sixth chapter should be in England. And that's that.' I pushed past him, and a branch of vine leaves flapped first into my face and then sprang back to do the same to Adam. We looked at each other, our faces streaming now with rain water, and burst out laughing.

'Holy Moly, you are one wet and beautiful Princess. There's a famous photo of Garbo, her face running with rainwater.' Adam pulled out his camera and took a photo of me. I pulled my hand up to my face, but I was, as usual, too late.

'Only you would think to take a photo right now and could you please try and get over your obsession that I look like Greta Garbo.' I walked on, so wet now that it didn't seem to matter. 'I just want to get to the top of the slope and look back down to the manor house.'

'I know, I know, but you even walk like Garbo... that long-legged easy stride. Did you ever see the film Ninotchka? A really early talkie, 1939, I think and with a great witty script by Billy Wilder. Hey, wait for me, Princess.'

I had drawn ahead of him, increasing my pace a little, 'Well, this is hardly the time to begin a discussion on film history. I just want to get out of the rain now.'

'OK, I know I bore you with talk of the great Garbo, but I'm going to make you watch some of her films... one day. But I agree, let's walk faster and get back to dry land. It's like an ocean of mud out here. I can't think why you wanted to walk around the vineyards in this weather. But, I know, once you set your mind on something, there's no stopping you.'

'Well, you didn't have to come with me.'

'Oh, but I did. I am your humble and obedient servant, Princess, you know that.'

'Give over, Adam, and can you please try, once again to drop the Princess tag… it's so vulgar. Anyway, admit it, you wanted to see the view, too.'

'True, my posh Princess, how can I stop calling you Princess when only a Princess would think it vulgar? No need to give a regal answer. Not sure there will be much view today. It is a lot wetter underfoot than I had imagined. How do they ever get grapes to turn into wine in this earth and this climate?'

'Well, it's all a matter of grape varieties, you see…'

'Forget I asked, no need to anser that either. I must be mad to lay myself open to a wine lecture right now. It would just about be the finishing touch to a perfect morning.'

'I'm surprised you're not more interested after all the time you have spent in vineyards over the last few months.'

'It's not the grapes that keep me going.'

We reached the top of the hill at that moment, and Adam looked down at me, his eyes strangely even bluer than usual. 'You know I just love being with you, Eve and once this effing book is finished, I think… well…'

To my extreme annoyance, his words were interrupted by the strident ringtone of my mobile. We often reached this point, half-discussing how we would stick to our working relationship until the book was completed. Echoing in my head was my father's voice saying, never mix business with pleasure. But why should I be listening to him? My phone was still bleeping and I searched in my pocket to turn it off… but then I saw that the caller was Bernard.

'It's Bernard,' I looked at Adam apologetically, 'I'd better answer it.'

'Yes, yes, of course.' Adam looked away from me and began to fiddle with the settings on his light meter.

'I'm going to take some shots from here. The mist forming in the valley around the manor is simply perfect.'

We both nodded, and I think we registered between us that the moment was lost and that we should carry on working… as always.

'Bernard says if we walk on over the crest of the hill that we can walk down to the road to the village and he'll pick us up there. He says it's nearer than trudging all the way back to the manor.'

'Good old Bernie, playing the trusty St Bernard dog. I'm surprised he doesn't appear any moment with a keg of brandy round his neck.'

'I know, he's always my saviour. Funny you should say that because I think he did start his career in the Alpine police force.'

'He never talks much about himself, does he.'

I thought about it for a moment. 'No,' I replied slowly, 'I suppose not, but then neither do we, do we?'

Adam walked ahead of me and then turned around and held out his hand, offering me a butterscotch sweet. I talk it from him gratefully, he always had a sweet in his Parka pocket. Maybe, one day, I would tell Adam of the strange coincidence... that it was also a habit of my father's to have an inexhaustible supply of butterscotch. I popped the sweet into my mouth and enjoyed the honeyed taste. My wine-tasting training had made me very conscious of flavours but now, this melting sweetness… yes, buttery with a suspicion of vanilla and salt… this was pure reminiscence. Yes, maybe when we had more time together without work, I would tell Adam about this unsettling and yet comforting connection with my childhood.

Adam continued to walk backwards as he spoke.

'Well, you certainly don't, and I suppose I don't either… not that there's much to say about my life.'

'Well, that's complete rubbish. You've had an amazing life already… and such success as a photographer.'

'Dragging myself out of the slums, you mean? Yeah, well, that's not very interesting, is it? I suppose it's just about the opposite of your life. Rags to riches and riches to rags and we end up the best of friends.'

I was about to reply, but before I could think of the right thing to say, Adam tripped and fell over backwards into the mud. Our contemplative little conversation turned instantly to helpless laughter.

I helped Adam up from the muddy ground, and we walked on together, arm in arm, downhill to where we could see Bernard had parked his gleaming limousine, waiting for us.

We began laughing all over again, when we saw Bernard's look of dismay at Adam's wet and muddy clothes.

'I think you can not be in my car, Adam. Look at you. Even you, Eve, you are very, very wet, I think.'

'I know, Bernard, but it's all my fault.' I said, 'I had no idea the land would be so water-logged, and I wanted to walk the extent of the vines. Adam thought he'd get a long shot of the manor. It all went rather wrong, although it's not my fault that Adam decided to walk backwards.'

Bernard shook his head and looked at us as though we were two naughty children as Adam and I tried, unsuccessfully, to stop laughing.

'No problem, Bernie.' Adam shook his long, wet hair, 'Look, I'll just take my Parka off. It's like wearing a waterproof tent.' Adam pulled his soaking wet Parka over his head, turning it inside out and rolled it up neatly. 'You see, I'm bone dry underneath.' He raised his hands up to the sky, and I blinked and then closed my eyes briefly. The rain had stopped suddenly, and Adam stood in a ray of sunlight. Bone dry and... yes, so like a Greek god that I decided I wouldn't look for too long. What had he said? The best of friends? When I opened my eyes again and had regained my equilibrium I found that Adam had begun to take his boots off and Bernard was holding out to me the spare loafers that I kept in the boot.

'Do you not want to change your shoes, Mademoiselle Eve?'

'Good idea, Bernard, *merci bien*. And I'll take off my Burberry.' I unbuttoned my long raincoat slowly, and Bernard stood behind me ready to take it from my shoulders. I arched my back, suddenly glad that I was wearing my favourite grey silk shirt and very gratified to see that Adam had his blue eyes narrowed, watching me carefully. Just the best of friends? Hmm.

'So, what did you think of our vines? I'm impressed you walked right through the whole vineyard.'

We were sitting at lunch with the Fellowes, the owners of the manor and its vineyards. Fortunately, it was an informal meal, taken in the huge kitchen and served straight from the Aga by Sara Fellowes. I had taken an instant liking to Sara and her husband, Hugo. They were perfect hosts, hospitable and well-mannered enough to ignore Adam's bare feet under their long refectory table. We had already tasted the last year's vintage, and I was struggling to find something good to say about it. The Fellowes' white wine was a dismal and very bland blend of Bacchus and Angevine grapes. I decided to compliment them on their vineyard instead,

'The vines look very healthy indeed. But it must be quite a struggle, I mean, the soil is so heavy.'

Sara placed a large rectangular dish of lasagne on the table and sat beside me. There is a saying I heard once, "If your soil won't grow wheat, grow apples, if your soil won't grow apples, grow soft fruit, if your soil won't grow soft fruit, grow grass and if that fails you, you can always grow vines." I think it's possibly true.' She laughed and began to dish out generous slices of the lasagne. 'As I'm sure you know, Eve, grapevines will grow pretty well anywhere, but if the soil is very fertile, then there will be too much leaf and not enough fruit. Where my family come from the land is so poor and gravelly that grapes are about the only thing that will come to harvest.'

'Where are your family from?' I looked at Sara in surprise as she seemed to be the archetypal English woman, complete with pale blue cashmere twinset and pearls.

'My family have roots in Tuscany, but I know very little about them. My grandparents came over to England to work as a gardener and cook for Lady Emily Hamilton, a rich single woman who owned this manor. When she died, my grandparents were amazed to find that she had left them the entire estate. My grandmother determined to create a vineyard on the south-facing slopes, up to where you walked today. My own mother, their only child, left the estate to me ten years ago when she died, sadly rather young. Luckily for me, I had already met and married dear Hugo. He rode into my life like a brave knight on a white horse.' Sara looked across at Hugo, and I saw the exchange of such a loving glance that it made me hold my breath for a moment. I looked at Adam and saw that he was as entranced with Sara's story as I was.

Hugo poured me a glass of wine and then took up the story. 'Sara always says that!' He laughed and reached out a hand and patted Sara's shoulder. 'What she means is that I turned up out of the blue when my old white Porsche had broken down almost on her baronial doorstep. She took me in and called for a mechanic and well, it was just love at first sight for both of us.'

Now Sara spoke again, 'And Hugo forgets to mention that he just happens to be the cleverest of men and a brilliant bio-chemist. The estate here was floundering into poverty, and he pulled the whole place round. Not just the vineyard, but by creating an overall business plan which involved his wine tours and wine-tasting evenings and my cookery courses.'

'None of which would have worked without Sara's brilliant ideas, too. Her cookery classes are always fully booked throughout the year. As far as your question, Eve, about the struggle, well, of course, you are quite right. It is a struggle but not one that can't be won. You can have success with the clay loam that we have here on the south and south-west facing slopes. We've no frost pockets and the foliage dries off quickly enough in the mornings to reduce the risk of fungal disease. Winter low temperatures are not a problem when the vines are dormant, even down to minus fifteen is tolerable. The problem is more at the pink bud stage, in the late Spring, then the vines are frost sensitive, and we have, once or twice, had to cover the vines with fleece... a bit costly but not impossible to manage.'

'Hugo is so very clever at judging when the weather is turning. Just this morning he said that the rain would ease up by lunch time and look out there.' Sara pointed to the window where the sun was shining through the fronds of wisteria.

Indeed, there was a glimmer of pale sunlight glancing through the tall window and casting a golden light on the smiling faces of Sara and Hugo Fellowes. It was all just a bit too much, somehow. There seemed to be no end to the Fellowes' mutual admiration, and I was beginning to wonder if it could all be too good to be true. Bernard who had been sitting quietly at the end of the table was perhaps sharing my cynicism, as he said,

'Is a beautiful story, Mrs Fellowes, and you do, indeed, live in a very lovely place. The lasagne was excellent. I think you have definitely inherited the Italian genius for cooking. Thank you, but if you will excuse me, I need to clean my car now. The weather has certainly improved.'

'Are you sure, Bernard? I have some peaches in white wine in the Aga.' Sara half-stood and smiled at Bernard.

'Thank you again, Mrs Fellowes, but I do not have sweet teeth. *Excusez-moi, s'il vous plaît.*'

Bernard stood up, gave a little bow and made his escape. I smiled across the table at Adam. I know we were both thinking that Bernard always knew the right moment to leave anything like a party.

We finished the lasagne and then a lightly dressed, lemony green salad. Sara telling us, with what was becoming a rather fixed tense smile, that they grew all their own fruit and vegetables. She then went on to tell how both their children were away at university. I was not at all surprised to learn that they were both expected to easily achieve honours degrees. Their son, following his father with a biochemistry degree at Durham and their daughter studying History of Art at Bath. More and more, the Fellowes dialogue seemed to be a well-rehearsed presentation of success. Could it all be quite so perfect?

Was there any fly to be found in the ointment at the Manor?

Certainly, the white peaches were baked to caramelised perfection, and I had no real reason to doubt anything.

'Holy Moly, you were well out of it, sitting in the car, Bernie. I mean, I've heard some boring wine talk since working with Eve, but this afternoon took the biscuit. The charming Fellowes are such jolly good fellows… really, they do protest too much, methinks, that their life is perfect, and everything in the state of Denmark and their Suffolk vineyard is drop-dead lovely.'

We were back in the Mercedes, and Adam was sitting in the front beside Bernard as we drove back to the Royal Park Hotel. Bernard glanced at me in the rear-view mirror and raised his dark eyebrows, completely baffled.

'You took biscuits? The vines are from Denmark or…'

I sharply interrupted Bernard,'What Adam is trying to say, idiomatically and with just about the worst misquotes I have ever heard, even from him, is that Sara and Hugo Fellowes seemed very anxious to tell us that life at the Manor and their work with their vineyards is very successful.'

'Ah, yes, I understand, I think. Is true, they are both very anxious to impress you, Eve. *Peut-être*, maybe is because they want the good publicity.'

'Hmm, probably,' I looked out of the window at the darkening landscape, 'I expect you're right, Bernard. And I agree with you, Adam, it was a long and tiring afternoon. The wines are boringly similar and they produce very little. Hugo is clearly obsessed with the chemical balance in the wine. Somehow there doesn't seem to be any guts or feeling to it. Anyway, sorry to keep you waiting so long, Bernard.'

'Oh, no problem at all. It is what my job involves. Anyway, I had a long telephone call with Elaine.'

Adam, who had been busily writing in his battered black notebook, looked up quickly,

'Did you, Bernie? So how is your long-distance love affair?'

Bernard sighed and ignored Adam then said, 'She sends you both her best wishes. The weather is still very hot in Roussillon, and she has full bookings with guests. She is very busy.'

'Does she miss you, Bernie?' Adam continued with his relentless teasing, and I felt sorry for Bernard although he was quite able to handle Adam. On our last assignment, in Frascati, when Adam had gone too far bantering and joking, Bernard had simply tipped Adam into the splashing waters of a fountain. I smiled at the memory. Adam did seem to have a habit of ending up wet and bedraggled. Now, he was sitting in the front, barefoot, and I was surprised when he asked Bernard to stop the car.

'Let me out here, Bernie, I'll walk the rest of the way back.'

Bernard pulled into a small sandy lay-by, and Adam jumped out. 'See you back at the Royal Park... is it dinner at the French Bistro tonight? My treat this time.'

Bernard leant across the car, 'Adam, have you noticed you have no shoes. Do you not want to take them from the boot?'

Adam looked down at his feet as though in surprise. 'Oh, yeah, good idea, Bernie. Hold on a mo, then. Yeah, I may as well put them on. Thanks.'

He ran round to the back of the car, and I turned to look through the back window. I saw he had pulled out his muddy Parka and was pulling it on as he pushed his feet into his boots. I shook my head in some sort of despair at how happy he looked. He saw me looking and raised his hand to wave, smiling his usual lopsided smile. Then he slammed the boot closed, waved once more and tapped on the side of the car in farewell. Bernard started up the car, and we moved forward. I remained looking out of the rear window, watching Adam striding out, his Parka flying loose in the light breeze. He looked glad to be on his own in the fresh air after our long afternoon. I understood that. I thought back to the long solitary hours I had spent in my beautiful farmhouse in Provence, quiet, happy hours whiling away the day writing poetry. But a small part of me wished he had asked me to join him, although I knew that I would have refused if he had asked me. I was definitely too sensible to want to walk any further through the rain-soaked Suffolk meadows and woods. Much too sensible.

I sighed and settled back into the comfort of the pale, grey leather seat, pulling over my knees the soft cashmere rug that Bernard always kept folded on the back seat. This was the luxury that I was accustomed to and found hard to live without. Adam had been right when he said that our lives were very different. I leant forward and spoke to Bernard.

'You know, Adam can't resist teasing you about Elaine, he's only joking. I suppose it's sort of English humour. You mustn't take offence, Bernard.'

'*Bien sur*, Mademoiselle Eve. I understand, *je sais, il me taquine. Moi aussi*, I am not serious to be angry with him. But as we have said before, Adam is irrepressible... is same word in French, *il est irrépressible, n'est ce pas?*'

'Oh yes, absolutely, irrepressible.' I looked again out of the window and silently wondered if a better word would be irresistible. 'He's come a long way in a short time. He has such amazing energy. I'm not surprised he has had outstanding success in his career.'

'True, he has the vital energy and great talent to capture human emotion in his photos. I begin to realise how famous he is... not just in London, *tu sais*, my son went to his exhibition in Paris recently. Is why that young boy wanted his autograph last night, *non*?'

'Yes, yes of course. His exhibition at the Imperial War museum of his Afghan war photos made a big noise, too. He is certainly super successful now.'

'Is why you have many fights, *non*?'

I turned away from watching the landscape roll past and looked at the familiar back of Bernard's solid neck. 'Fights? What do you mean, Bernard?' My voice sounded higher than usual, as I was so surprised.

'You know, arguing often. *Vous vous disputez souvent... mais*, but just the little fights.'

I felt my cheeks flushing at the thought that Bernard was, in some gentle way, telling me off. 'Oh, I know we often row, but it doesn't last long. Sometimes I don't even know why it starts.'

'Often is because you not think him equal, I think.'

'Equal?' I was still staring at the back of Bernard's neck, and my voice was still higher than usual. 'What do you mean?'

'*Alors*, I think is difficult for you both. For me, is simple. I work for you, Mademoiselle Eve, even though now you like me to call you Eve. But is simple that I work for you. For Adam is very different. He is already important photographer, and he is working with you. I hope my English is correct, is same in French, *non*? *Il travaille avec vous, il ne travaille pas pour vous.* Please excuse me.'

'Nothing to excuse, Bernard.' I replied slowly and my voice seemed to have dropped to its usual timbre. 'I think I understand. In fact, I think you have explained it very well. Thank you. I'll think about it, I promise.'

I remained silent, then, thinking about thinking.

8

Dinner, that night in the French bistro, was a jolly affair. I think we were all pleased that the long, rainy day was over and satisfied with our efforts. I had a full pad of hand-written notes ready to be sorted out on my laptop and elaborated into something of an interesting account. Adam had already shown us a whole batch of excellent photographs, all atmospherically misty. It seemed as though, for once, our work might be quickly over.

Adam looked at Bernard and then to me, 'That was a good day's work. I'm pleased with my photos of today's gentle but moody landscape.' Adam smiled, a satisfied, almost smug lop-sided grin as he finished his entrecôte. I laughed at him, saying,

'You do realise you are always pleased with yourself, don't you?'

'Well, pleased with my photography at least. Not always so pleased with myself.'

I was puzzled by his answer but could think of no particular response, so I tutned to Bernard, 'Do you know, I think we might actually have an easy assignment this time?'

Bernard nodded and raised, 'Is time you had an easy assignment, *n'est ce pas*?'

I raised my glass of rather good Fleurie, 'I'll drink to that. I shall just do my best with the Fellowes' perfect life and their boring wines. If Suffolk is what my publishers want then, I'll give it to them. Yes, this should be an easy chapter.'

Adam clinked his glass of water to mine and then to Bernard, who, for once had joined me in a glass of the delicious young Beaujolais. Normally, wanting to be ready to drive, he abstained from alcohol. Maybe, he too, had decided our work might already be over. Now, as he laid his glass back on the table he said quietly,

'I think I have found your Irish man.'

Adam and I put down our glasses quickly and the mood at the table suddenly darkened. We both stared at Bernard as he continued, his voice very low,

'Is difficult for me with the accents, but I am sure it was your man. I was cleaning the car in the garages behind the hotel, when a man called out to another who was backing out.'

Backing out?' Adam asked, his voice sounding hopeful, 'Has he gone then?'

'*Non, non*, both men got into the car and then I heard them say something about horses… and if I understood something about a ring. Then I watched as they drove to the front of the hotel and parked again.'

'A ring?' I looked at Bernard in surprise but kept my voice low, feeling nervously unsettled. 'Surely it can have nothing to do with me. Why a ring?'

'I am nearly certain they talked of ring and again they spoke of Eve Sinclair.' Bernard shrugged, 'Was difficult to hear and understand.'

'But the car, Bernie, you saw the car? You'd know it again?'

Bernard gave Adam a withering look, 'Not difficult, Adam, was a silver Ferrari 4.5 Spider convertible, two-door, Scuderia Ferrari Shields, Alcantara Inner Wheel Arches, high spec interior, black leather with hand-stitching.'

Adam raised his eyebrows and then said with a quick flash of a smile, 'Is that all you noticed, Bernie? Didn't you even get the registration plate number?'

'*Bien sur*, MIK 3636, is a special number. I wait now for a call from friend of mine in London Metropolitan Police. He will tell me the owner name.'

Now both Adam and I were looking at Bernard in stunned silence, and so he carried on again, 'You know I have many friends in the police. One time, many years ago now, I worked on a drugs case in London. It was linked with a crime in Paris. So, no problem, I called this old friend in London. Soon I hear from him, *bien sur*.'

Adam gave a soft whistle as he scribbled in his small black notebook, 'You're the man, Bernie, man of the day.'

I nodded in agreement and then said, 'But why do we care about this Irish guy. Maybe he is a villain but nothing to do with us. I think we should keep well away from him and his friend… and his silver Ferrari.'

'Hold on Princess, it was you that first told us you heard this Paddy say your name.'

'I know, but what on earth can it matter? All he said was something about it all being impossible now that Eve Sinclair was here. I don't understand why.'

Adam shook his head, 'I don't know either, unless it's something to do with the media interest that follows you around. I mean, if you're planning to do something crooked, then you wouldn't want any extra attention, would you? If they are villains, as you said, Princess. Like the word, by the way, villain… sounds like something out of a Sherlock Holmes story.'

'Do you indeed, well it's a perfectly good and very ancient word, 14th century if not earlier and derived from the old French word *vilain* meaning peasant or farmer, which, of course, comes from the Medieval Latin *villanus*… farmhand but...'

Adam interrupted me, 'Of course, of course, I knew that. You know, Princess, sometimes I think you should have stayed in the sheltered halls of academia. Are you actually fit for this world?'

I looked at him in surprise, 'It's only a fact. I'm interested in words, that's all.'

'I don't know how you put up with my slangy crumby English and Bernard's Franglais. Do you quietly laugh at us?'

'Don't be ridiculous, Adam.' I felt the familiar jab of anger inside me and then I remembered Bernard's words to me earlier. I took a deep breath, 'It would be just the same if you spoke to me about photography… you must know so much about depth of field or light exposure… things I can't even begin to understand.'

To my surprise, I saw that Adam was looking at his empty plate and actually blushing with what could have been pleasure or even embarrassment. I glanced at Bernard to see if he had noticed my attempt to mollify Adam, but he was not looking at me. His head was held low, but his brown eyes, dark and piercing, were looking up and across the restaurant as two men came in and sat at a table.

Adam looked at Bernard and he said very quietly.

'Are they the guys you saw in the Ferrari, Bernie?'

'Yes, *bien sur.* Do not look at them. Here, look at the menu and keep talking and laughing. And you, Eve.'

Adam and I did as we were told and had an animated discussion over the choice between *Tarte Tatin* or *Îles Flottantes*. Bernard stood up,

'*Eh bien*, I have eaten very much. I leave you two young people to choose a dessert. I shall make some phone calls and see you later or tomorrow.' He nodded, and I tried to guess what he meant. I felt ridiculously scared but tried to speak normally,

'Are you sure, Bernard? Give my love to Elaine and let me know if you have any news from your friend in London.'

'*Bien sur*, Mademoiselle Eve. *Bonsoir* Adam.'

'Don't you want me to… er… join you, Bernie? Take a walk round the block?' Adam half rose from his seat.

Bernard shook his head firmly. '*Non, non.*' Then he leant closer to us, 'I watch and wait a little outside, is easy for a chauffeur.' Then, in a louder voice, '*Bonne soirée!*' Before we could say anything more, he turned quickly on his heel and left the restaurant looking neither right nor left.

The waiter arrived at our table, and we quickly ordered one of each of the desserts on the menu, having little interest in either. As soon as the waiter had left our side, Adam spoke,

'Bernard is something else, isn't he? Is he actually a bodyguard as well as a chauffeur? I mean, do you think that's why your father employed him?'

'I don't know,' I shrugged, feeling uncomfortable talking about my father and the past. 'Maybe. Well, yes, I suppose so.'

Adam appeared to sense my unease and carried on quickly, 'Anyway, he's a great mate. I'm so pleased to have met him.'

'I'm sure he feels the same. Only this afternoon, after you jumped out of the car, he was praising you and said how irrepressible you are.'

'Irrepressible? Is that a good thing then? My old man wouldn't think so. He was always trying to bash me down, often literally. Just imagine if I'd had a father like Bernard.'

I blinked at the very idea of how my own life would have been so different if Bernard had been my father. Of course, my own father had been undeniably a good provider of anything that money can buy, but had he bestowed me with real security? Then, I struggled to remember that it was Adam that had suffered actual deprivation of love, and I answered quickly, 'Who knows… maybe you've only done so well because of fighting adversity.'

'I love it when you talk posh, Princess. Villains and adversity… you're wasting your time writing about wine. You should write thrillers.'

'I think it's best to write about what you know. I know nothing about criminal life, nothing at all.'

'True, best it stays that way, in my opinion.'

I was silent for a minute, thinking that my own father had been labelled a criminal in some of the newspapers only a year or so ago. I was sure that Adam hadn't thought about it at all, but I felt uneasy again. Adam reached out and put his hand lightly over mine.

'So, Princess Piglet, are you going for the upside down tart or the floating islands? You can choose.'

'Let's eat half of each and then swap.' I replied, not moving my hand, enjoying the dry warmth of his hand on my skin. He smiled at me, a sweet smile that was unusually not lop-sided. Then the waiter arrived with the two desserts. I looked down at the Tarte Tatin that he had placed in front of me, and took up my spoon and made a small dig at it. The crumbly pastry, coated with the glistening sweet apple, divided easily into a small morsel. I put it neatly on my spoon and offered it to Adam. He looked at me and opened his mouth obediently and then closed his eyes as he savoured the soft sweetness. I took a small breath as I watched his long, golden lashes brush his cheeks.

Why did I have to worry about Irish accents and English manor houses? There was so much more to life… right in front of me… but then, it was impossible to ignore the bad feeling I had about the two men on the other side of the restaurant. I glanced across and saw they were both staring at me.

9

'Would you be Eve Sinclair, the TV girl?'

To my dismay, the two men that I had just caught rudely staring straight at me, had now walked across the restaurant and come right up to our table. I felt Adam's hand close tighter over mine, and he answered for me.

'You're quite correct, sir, this is Eve Sinclair and who might you be?' Adam's voice was friendly but firm enough to demand an answer. My heart was thumping in my ears as I struggled to remain calm. The man that had spoken had a strong Irish accent, and he was staring at me again, so close now that I could see the pores of his heavy skin and the shadow of a beard. He carried on looking at me, and I had the sudden realisation that he was trying to intimidate me. I gave him an icy glare followed by the benefit of one of my best professional smiles. I had never been one to be bullied.

The man quickly looked down, unable to keep eye contact, and he hesitated, then said, 'My name's not important at all, but I was wondering if I could ask for your autograph, Miss Sinclair? I've seen you on the telly, of course.'

'Really, which programme sticks in your mind? I always think it's interesting to know.' My voice sounded as cold as ice in my ears.

Now the man was really floundering, his face turning a dark purplish red of confusion. A Burgundy or heart attack red, I thought to myself, as I waited for him to stumble out his reply.

'Well, now, that would be asking, wouldn't it? They're all as good as each other in my humble opinion.' He was recovering his pace now, and I wondered if this was the famous Irish blarney. 'My good wife will be thrilled to know I've met you, that's for sure.'

'Really, so your wife watches, too?'

'Oh yes, we haven't missed a night.'

'Well, thank you, I always thought it surprising that the programmes went out on a Tuesday.

'Oh, we looked forward to it every Tuesday, to be sure.'

I looked away then, tired of testing him out and hearing his obvious lies. My programmes had always held a prime Saturday evening slot. Then Adam spoke up,

'Are you here for the races?'

'Yes, yes, it should be a fine weekend. We shall have a whale of a time, to be sure.'

'Are you staying at the Royal Park?' Adam asked, his voice still friendly and casual.

'No, no... it's a bit pricey for us. We're staying in town.'

'Where are you from? Have you come over from Ireland?'

Now the second man took hold of the Irishman's arm and gave it a small tug. 'Come on now, Mick, this is all very pleasant, but we have to get going. A pleasure to meet you, Miss Sinclair.' His voice was smooth and self-assured with an average London accent.

The man we now knew as Mick, stood up straight and patted his brightly striped tie. 'Indeed, indeed we do. A fine evening to you both.'

And then they were gone, making their way hastily to the exit, without any further mention of my autograph.

I moved my hand away from Adam's and ran my fingers through my hair, feeling the tension leave my shoulders.

'Well, that was a ridiculous conversation.' I looked at Adam, and we both almost laughed.

'I thought so, too. Although there was something very unpleasant about them both. The Irishman was not as smooth as his friend, but he looked like a typical bully. I liked the way you stood up to him.'

'Well, I could tell he thought he was in charge of the conversation. I couldn't have that, could I?'

'That's my Princess, always in charge.' Adam laughed, and I tried to smile although I was not sure I quite liked the inference. But he continued before I could respond, 'The other guy was a lot smoother, and I'm sure he realised that his Irish mate was about to say too much. Then, he gave away Mick's name. I mean if they were trying to hide anything, that wasn't very smart. Hmm, but I'd say they are definitely up to something and for some reason it involves you. I mean, they certainly didn't want your autograph.'

'I know, nor had Mick and his good wife ever watched my programmes.'

'Hmm, he slipped easily into your little trap, didn't he?' Adam finished the last morsel of his dessert and then looked at me in dismay. 'Oh, God, sorry Eve. I was supposed to share my pud, wasn't I It seemes to have floated right down my throat?'

'Oh, don't worry, I'm completely full up. You can finish off mine, if you want? Look, there's Bernard coming back into the restaurant now.'

Bernard sat down at the table, and the waiter came over and took our order for coffee. As soon as he had gone, I turned to Bernard,

'Any news from your police friend, Bernard? We've just had a silly conversation with the two men.'

'Yes, yes, I was watching from the side window. I saw you talking to them, and yes, my friend, Colin, has found the name of the owner of the Ferrari. His name is Michael Flanagan, and his address is in Kilburn. I have it correctly on a text.'

'You're the man, Bernie. I didn't even notice you were watching us through the window.'

'Was the idea, Adam. I didn't want you two giving any idea I was involved. I was just ready to come in if... *alors*, well, if you needed help.'

Adam laughed and slapped Bernard on the back, 'Ever-ready, Saint Bernard, to rescue the Princess. Good thing, too. In fact, both men were aggressive in their own way. Mick the Irishman seemed an obvious bully, but Eve faced him down magnificently. The oily Londoner was more menacing in his own quiet way. I didn't like the look of either of them. Any funny business and I would have taken on the Englishman, but Mick looks a convincing heavyweight.'

'I agree, Adam,' Bernard nodded, 'I've seen you in action before, but men like that... you must beware. They may carry knives or guns.

'Oh, for goodness sakes, you two.' I shook my head in impatience, 'I think you're making too much out of this. They may be crooks but...'

Adam interrupted me, 'Crooks or villains, maybe Eve, but I really don't understand why they are interested in you.'

'Exactly.' Bernard nodded and sipped the last of his small black coffee. '*Exactement*, this is the point. Why they talk of you, Eve? Also, I am thinking while I wait... do you, *par hazard*, by chance, have a valuable ring with you? Remember I heard them talk of a ring, too.'

'Regrettably not, Bernard. The ring my father gave me on my twenty-first, the blue diamonds, was one of the first things I sold when things went so wrong. I suppose I never really liked it anyway.'

'Tt, tt,' Bernard looked at me sadly and with a frown of disapproval. 'Is very sad shame. Your father bought that ring for you in Hatton Garden. I remember waiting for him that day. He was a very long time choosing it.'

'Well, it wasn't as though I wanted to sell it. It's just too bad.' I answered defiantly, but I felt sick at heart at the thought of the little hoop of diamonds now probably on another woman's finger.

'Was it very valuable?' Adam asked, 'I mean would a thief know you had it once?'

'I suppose so, quite possibly. But then they'd have to be pretty stupid not to know that I had sold it at Christie's.'

'Well, neither of the men seemed particularly clever. Cunning and greedy maybe, but I wouldn't say they were as sharp as marbles. The English guy even gave Mick's name away. The last thing anyone would do if they were pulling a trick.'

'True, I think they'd both had a fair bit to drink, as well.' I sighed, 'I know the signs only too well. They were both a bit bleary. I had thought maybe Mick wasn't his real name. I mean, it could be a nickname, but it seems to match Bernard's research. Michael Flanagan. There can't be a more Irish name in the whole of Ireland, and it sounds made-up to me, but if the Ferrari is registered and with the Kilburn address then...' I hesitated, speaking my thoughts aloud and not sure of anything. 'And, then, why would they say they weren't staying here? I heard them in that room near mine.'

Bernard stood up, 'Is very true. I watched them go to reception desk, and they have two rooms on the first floor. Twenty-two and twenty-three. I saw them collect their room cards and then they took the lift.' Bernard nodded and then looked down at us both and said suddenly, 'Why you say silly conversation?'

I was silent as I thought about that. If it had been silly, then why had I felt so threatened?

10

The next day I took breakfast in my room. I had told Bernard and Adam that I would meet them for coffee about eleven as I wanted to work on my notes. I was still anxious about the quality of the Fellowes' wines, and how I would write about them.

My room had a small balcony that overlooked the hotel gardens and across to the stabling of a stud. The early morning sun was quite strong, and I enjoyed the peace of being alone. It was one of the big disadvantages of my TV work that I found hard to get used to. More and more, wherever I went, people recognised me and stared. I knew that I should accept the fact and smile my way through, as Melanie, my loyal media agent, advised and frequently begged me to do. I had tried over my week in London, and I had even practised smiling in the mirror. I had developed a quick flashing smile that could possibly be called radiant. At least, that is what the media termed the way my facial muscles creased... but now I wanted to relax. Being stared at by the public was one thing, but the hard glares of the two men last night at dinner were quite another.

I turned off my mobile and enjoyed the peace... small birds singing in the tall trees, the distant sound of guests on the terrace and nothing I needed to worry about. I watched the horses being walked through the stable yard next door. The sound of their hooves on the cobbles rang out, and there was a whiff of the stable in the air. I breathed in, not at all displeased by the smell. I had spent some of the happiest hours of my childhood on horseback in Hyde Park, changing as I grew, from the smallest of ponies to my last horse, a beautiful chestnut hunter. The hunter had been the last thing I had sold, just a few months after my diamond ring. I leant on the balcony rail and thought sadly about that time. Everything had changed when my father had disappeared in the maelstrom of financial disaster. Now, I knew I was still struggling to keep my head above the stormy waters even as I tried to appear in control. I blinked back tears of self-pity as I thought about my father so far away. Tears of self-pity and anger. How could he desert me and leave me to fend for myself in this alien world of working for money? Why had he spoilt me so much that I found it so hard to cope with what I now found was such a different everyday life? He had always given me everything I wanted and then everything I had never even dreamed about. Everything from horses to diamonds. I brushed the tears from my eyes and looked at my hands, bare of any rings. Had the two men actually planned to steal my ring? It seemed an impossible idea. First, the ring was of such importance, that Christies had featured it on the cover of their auction catalogue. It was a very valuable piece of Russian antique jewellery and had sold for a high price. The smallest time spent on research would show that I no longer owned it. Surely, any criminal would have checked its history? I sighed with impatience as then I thought of another flaw in Bernard's idea. Yes, secondly, why would they have said it was hopeless now that Eve Sinclair was here? Obviously ridiculous. No, it had to be something other than that. Adam was more likely to be right when he had suggested that my presence created too much media commotion. I sighed again, more heavily as I struggled with this idea. It was so much easier to hide out in my comfortable suite and enjoy some solitude.

I flicked my laptop open and began to cobble together the start of an article on the Fellowes wines. I had collated all the information and, now I just wanted to get the bare bones of a theme that I could plump out later. Sara Fellowes had invited us to tea and a tour of the cellars. I picked up my laptop and went into the small lounge that was part of my suite. It was easier to work out of the sunlight and, an hour later, I had written more than I needed. I saved my work and then closed my laptop with some satisfaction. It wasn't brilliant but, it would do for a start. I poured myself a second orange juice and went back out into the sunshine. I stretched out on a sun-lounger, feeling drowsy and more relaxed than I had been earlier. I finished my juice and then began to breathe deeply and began some gentle yogic exercises, letting my stomach fill and empty with air, concentrating my mind on... nothing, nothing at all.

I was running, running as fast as I could but my legs were heavy as lead and I made no progress. I looked back over my shoulder, a strong side wind blew my hair over my face, but I could make out the two men running, gaining ground on me. I turned to look ahead, the sky was gunmetal grey and stormy, and I saw my chestnut horse tethered to a tall, dark tree. She whinnied anxiously, and I reached my hand out toward her, trying to catch hold of her mane, or the reins that were swinging loose. Now, I could hear the heavy footsteps of the men behind me, and I struggled to move but the earth was sinking away from my feet, and I was being drawn down into a quagmire. I tried to scream, but I could make no noise. I was powerless, completely powerless. My heart was beating in my chest like a caged bird, my ears were filled with a loud banging noise. Banging and banging, knocking louder...

.... and then I awoke. I lay, hot and confused and realised that someone was knocking on the door. I sat up on the sun-lounger, trying to gather my senses, my heart still thumping as slowly relief flooded through me. Of course, it was only a dream. I looked up at the cloudless gentle blue Suffolk sky and regained my equilibrium. Then, over the knocking noise I heard my name called, well, not really my name.

'Princess, Princess are you all right?'

I ran to the door, unlocked it and yanked it wide open. Adam almost fell into the room as he had obviously been leaning against the door. We collided and I breathed in the aroma that always clung around Adam. It was a perfume and yet not a perfume. It had been intriguing me ever since I first met him... or rather, first smelt him. My well-trained nose almost quivered with the effort of analysing the complex combination... definitely the ozone of the sea, maybe seaweed… but no, there was a strong minty overtone… peppermint or menthol, almost chewing gum… but then there was a background of honey, sweet as melting fudge. It was all so complicated and quite faint even when I was very close to him. Suddenly I realised I was clinging to him, as close as his perfume clung. Then, I was aware that I was wearing one of my father's shirts that I often wore for work. Nothing more. I stepped back quickly, and he did the same. We had sworn to each other that until this book was complete, we would not risk mixing work with pleasure. Adam was looking down at me, his face more serious than usual, his eyes bluer than ever and his cheeks flushed dark under his tan. For once, he seemed lost for words and then he said, in an unusually hoarse voice, exactly what I was thinking,

'Not to mix work with pleasure? But it would be such a pleasure, such a great pleasure.'

I turned reluctantly away from him, pulling the large man's shirt around me and shaking back my tousled hair. I didn't know how to answer him, and I was still recovering from my nightmare and… and being in Adam's comforting embrace, enveloped in his perfume. He continued, his voice more normal now, joking,

'You look dreadful, Princess. I've never seen you so hot and flustered before.'

'I fell asleep in the sun on the balcony.' His words had brought me back to reality with a bang, and I decided not to tell him about my nightmare.

'I've been calling your mobile over and over. I was worried about you. You're never late.'

'Late? What do you mean?' I flicked on my mobile and saw that there were seven missed calls from Adam. Worse than that, it was half past eleven. I must have been asleep for over an hour.

11

I made it down to the terrace on the south side of the hotel by noon. It was a perfect English summer's day, the lawns were fresh green from yesterday's rain, and sweet pink roses perfumed the air... but I was angry at myself for being late. Bernard and Adam were sitting at one of the tables under a large cream umbrella, drinking coffee and in conversation with a young man. A very handsome young man. Bernard and Adam stood up as I joined them and then the young man jumped up hastily. Bernard had, for some time now, led Adam into this old world courtesy, and I was always rather charmed by it. Did I want to be the sort of woman who had doors opened for her? It was a confusing idea, but I rather thought I did. Bernard smiled at me,

'I think now you begin to relax, Eve. Is good to be a little late sometimes.'

How was it that he always knew just the right and kind thing to say? I laughed and sat in the chair he was holding for me.

'Thank you, Bernard. I do apologise. I know I said we'd meet at eleven, but we don't have to be at the Fellowes' until teatime, so I suppose it doesn't really matter too much. I had thought to try another vineyard in Norfolk but... well, you're quite right, it's fine to be off schedule occasionally. Sorry, though.'

'Please, Eve, say no more. It has been a grand pleasure sitting here in this beautiful English garden. We have been talking with young Toni. Very interesting.'

I turned to look at the handsome newcomer sitting between Adam and Bernard, 'Ah, you must be the farrier that Adam told me about. Pleased to meet you.' I shook hands with the young man. His grip was noticeably strong, but he held my hand gently and flashed a perfect row of white teeth as he smiled. Farrier, maybe, but he could have easily been a film star.

'Pleased to meet you, Eve.' He fluttered dark, sooty eyelashes and looked at me with his brown, almost black, eyes. 'Of course, I would have known you anywhere, the famous Eve Sinclair, but my fiancée already told me that you're staying at the Park.'

'Ah, of course, I remember now. You're engaged to Lois. I met her in the Spa when I arrived.'

I did indeed remember, and that I had been cross that the young beauty therapist had talked about me to her boyfriend. I had remembered her name now, too, but I failed to conjure up an image of her. Maybe petite and possibly blonde? Toni was so good-looking, in an Italian way, that I found myself thinking that Lois was probably very pretty. Did couples match up to each other in attractiveness, and then... what about levels of intelligence? My mind fluttered around the possibility of Adam being my match on both counts. I looked at him then, trying to judge him impartially which, of course, was quite impossible. Then, I realised that the conversation had continued while I had been lost in my foolish thoughts. I homed in again in the middle of what Adam was saying,

'That would be great. What do you think, Eve? Lunch in a Suffolk pub? It would be an education for Bernard, don't you agree?'

I nodded vaguely, while I took in the idea and Adam continued, 'and Lois will be there, too. Well, Eve?'

Then I realised he was waiting for me to agree. Lunch in a pub? How could I possibly tell him that I had never done anything like it... not even when I was a student at Cambridge. I glanced at Bernard and saw he was looking at me with an amused smile. That made my mind up, and I answered quickly, 'Yes, yes, great idea.'

Adam nodded happily, and I was relieved that at least he hadn't guessed that a pub lunch was an unknown activity in my sheltered, wealthy life. I looked across to the gardens and then became aware that there was a group of women in animated conversation at the next table. I carefully avoided making any eye contact, as they were sure to have recognised me. If I were fortunate, then their good manners would save me from being asked for an autograph or just a conversation. I pulled on my dark sunglasses and sneaked a sidelong view at the women. They were all of a certain age, very well-groomed and obviously enjoying each other's company. There must have been seven or eight around the table, and I thought they were probably fresh from the spa. Whether from exercise or beauty treatments, they all had an aura of confidence and glamour. Their well-cut hair, mostly silvery blonde, shone in the sun and their skin glowed with health. I took another sneak look and thought how I should like to be like them when or if I reached that age. Age, now there was another thought. I looked at the table on the other side of us and saw a group of young women, possibly a hen party? They may have been young, but they had none of the confidence of the group of older women. They seemed to be over-dressed, almost to the point of pantomime costume, and they were screeching at each other but not listening at all. Suddenly one of them stood up, knocking over a bottle of champagne and several glasses. The girl, tottering on high-heeled sandals, began to scream and swear at another girl. They were both dressed in shocking pink and wearing feathery fascinators. Was the row about their similar outfits? Everyone on the terrace was now watching as the two girls shouted abuse at each other. Then, the first girl gave the other a small push and the other reacted sharply by pulling the other girl's hair and wrenching the fascinator from her head. Adam stood up, and I looked at him and saw to my surprise that he was laughing. The girls were now slapping and kicking at each other with all their might. Then, the double door to the terrace opened and David West, the concierge, glided quickly onto the scene. He stood beside the two girls and tried to calm the situation. Then Adam was there, and I saw him grab an ice bucket from the girl's table and tip the water and ice over the girls. The fight stopped immediately, and the two girls stood gasping, their hair in bedraggled rats' tails and black lines of mascara streaking down their cheeks. David West quietly led them both into the hotel, and the scene was over.

Adam made his way back to our table, smiling broadly. As he passed the table of older women they all clapped quietly, and he gave them a little bow. He stopped to talk to them for a while, and then I saw he had his camera in his hand and was taking a photo of the group. It was very obvious, even from my sidelong view, that the women were charmed by Adam. When finally he returned to our table, he was still laughing.

'Nothing like a good cat fight, is there?' He turned to me, 'I don't suppose your girlfriends ever behave like that, Eve? What a bunch of trouble, Essex girls up for a day's racing.'

'Oh, of course, they're here for the races. I thought perhaps it was a hen party.'

We sat quietly for a minute, finishing our coffee. I looked across the rolling green lawns and almost laughed aloud. How to tell Adam that I had never really had any girlfriends and certainly never seen what he called a cat fight... but then I had never been to a pub lunch with my chauffeur, my photographer, a masseuse and a farrier. There was always a first time for everything... or so I was discovering.

12

We were just pulling out of the gates to the hotel, following Toni in his van, when there was an insistent electronic beep from the control panel in front of Bernard. A silver Ferrari swung into the drive and Bernard pressed a button on his steering wheel and silenced the sound. Then pulled the Mercedes to a halt just outside the gates.

'I think to miss my education at pub lunch. I go back. Adam, you drive Eve to this pub, yes?'

I was sitting in the back, and Adam was sitting beside Bernard in the front. I was shocked that Bernard should even consider the idea.

'Wait a minute. What do you mean, Bernard?'

'Excuse me, Mademoiselle Eve, but is important I find more about the men in Ferrari. Is good chance.'

'Are you sure they are important? Why not leave them to whatever crooked thing they have in mind.'
Adam turned round and looked at me, frowning.

'I think Bernard is right. But I could go back and then, Bernard could drive you on to lunch.'
Bernard shook his head, 'Is not good plan, Adam. No, I go now.'
He opened the driver's door and held out the keys to Adam. 'You have driven before on our journey from Provence, just remember is automatic and drive slow, please.'

I leant forward and snatched the keys from Bernard.

'I'm perfectly capable of driving myself to a pub. Hurry up then, Bernard, out you get. Toni is waiting in a lay-by up ahead.'

I jumped out of the car, and Bernard held the driver's door open until I had adjusted the seat. Both men were silent, and I almost laughed at the thought that they knew better than to argue with me when I was determined about something. Maybe I did like old fashioned courtesy and the odd door held open for me, but there was no way I needed to be driven around like a child. Those days were long gone. I looked in the rear-view mirror as I pulled away, but there was no sign of Bernard. For a large man, he could certainly move quickly and secretly, and I suddenly felt worried.

'Do you think Bernard will be all right on his own? What was that beeping sound from the dashboard when the Ferrari passed us?' I flicked a glance at Adam who was sitting beside me and studying the small screen on his camera.

'I think Bernie has the Ferrari tracked or something. One of his gizmo ideas. Bernie will be OK. He knows very well how to look after himself. He has some idea up his sleeve, I guess.'

'I hate all this. I wish we could just ignore those men. I wish I'd never told you both that I heard them say my name.'

'Well, you did, so it's too late, and anyway, it's best to be careful. You're a precious commodity.'

'A commodity? That makes me sound like a useful product.'

'Oh, I wouldn't go as far as to say useful. But, all right, if it offends your majesty then stick with precious.'

I frowned at the road ahead, struggling not to respond. This was no time for one of our pointless arguments.

'Look, Toni's signalling to turn right.' Adam was leaning forward in his seat, stretching his seat belt. 'Signal to follow him, Eve.'

I gave a long, impatient sigh, 'I saw him signalling as we came over the hill. Would you please sit back and not be a backseat driver sitting in the front?'

'That's a very confusing princessy order, but I'll try.' Adam sat back in his seat and put his hands over his eyes. 'Is that OK?'

'Don't be ridiculous, Adam. Let's just have this lunch in a pub and try to enjoy it.'

'It's called a pub lunch not a lunch in a pub. I'm beginning to regret the whole idea.' Adam sighed now and returned to studying his camera. 'I could have taken some more photos at the hotel. The weather is perfect today, and I promised the manager I'd give them some shots for their website.'

'Really? Do you have time for that?'

'Do you mean do I have time when I should be working for you, your royal highness? Do I need to remind you that you were asleep in the sun when we had arranged to meet this morning at eleven?'

The conversation was definitely turning into one of our rows, and I gripped the steering wheel tightly as I tried to control my rising temper. I had not meant that Adam should work full time for me or with me. Or had I? Did I resent any time that Adam spent away from me? But why was that? Fortunately, I saw ahead that Toni was turning into the car park of a pub called the Black Horse. A very small car park. I manoeuvred the long limousine slowly into a space until the electronic warning beeped. Adam jumped out of the car and checked the front, then came round to my door and opened it,

'Very neat parking, Princess, in fact, you drive very well, I'd say you're a right royal driver.' He beamed at me cheekily, his usual crooked grin, and my temper dispersed completely.

Adam held the door of the pub open for me, and I walked in ahead of him. There was an embarrassing pause in the noisy talk. Everyone there seemed to be staring at me for a brief moment, and then conversations began again. I faltered, and Adam took my elbow and steered me through the close-packed room to where Toni was already sitting at a table in a corner. I felt my cheeks burning, and I sat quickly in the chair that Toni held out for me. Adam sat beside me,

'That happens everywhere she goes!' He spoke in a cheery voice and added, 'Just a bit more noticeable here.'

I remained silent, summing up his words and trying to regain my equilibrium. I realised there was a girl sitting close to Toni, holding his hand, and my well-trained manners kicked in at last,

'Hi, you must be Lois.' I gave one of my professional smiles and held out my hand. Too late I realised that it was a rather French thing to do. The girl looked as startled as a rabbit in the headlights, but offered me her hand.

'Yes, I'm Lois, Toni's fiancée.' She gave a quick glance to Toni as though wanting confirmation. Toni turned to her, and they held each other's eyes for a long moment. Adam took over,

'Well, this is a great pub. What will you have?' He turned to me, and I knew he thought I would have trouble thinking of what to drink. I answered quickly,

'Soda and lime, please, I'm driving.' I was very pleased with my answer as it made me sound as though I regretted not being able to drink beer. I had looked around the small tables and the long bar and noticed large tankards of a very dark brew. I might be a wine expert but I knew nothing much of anything that hops produced, apart from the fact that the dark frothy liquid didn't appeal to me in the least. Lois then ordered a shandy and Toni asked for half a lager. I knew Adam very rarely drank anything alcoholic, so it suddenly seemed rather silly to be sitting in this dark room. I cautiously looked around, not wanting to make eye contact with anyone likely to be a fan. The walls were of a very beautiful flint and brick, and the ceiling was low and heavily beamed. A collection of horseshoes decorated one white-washed wall. Ah, there was some excellent conversational material. I turned to Toni,

'Is that a collection of old horseshoes?'

He turned to look at them, 'Yes, and all from racehorses, you can tell by the shape.'

'You can, I can't! In fact, I often think horses look alike when they're the same colour. Where I used to ride there were a lot of chestnuts.' I smiled at him, and I was about to tell him about my own horse's distinctive three white socks and his nervousness when he was shod, but then, possibly fortunately, Adam returned with a tray of drinks.

'Cheers, it's good to get away from the five-star world for a while.' Adam raised his glass and smiled at us all and I thought that he really meant what he said. Did he find it stuffy or boring in my world? Was it my world or would I rather be alone in my Provencal *mas*, writing poetry again? I realised Adam was still talking,

'You mustn't mind, Eve is always drifting off into her very own dream world. She's in one of her reveries. I call them Evereveries.'

Lois smiled and then said quietly, 'You shouldn't tease, Adam. Eve needs time to be creative. All artists do. I know Eve is a famous TV celeb, now, but I've read all her articles, and she's a really good writer. She has a way of vividly making you feel as though you are right there in the vineyards. I'm a great fan.'

'Goodness, thank you, Lois. I wish I had stayed a writer and not gone over to TV. Being recognised everywhere is so difficult.'

Lois leant toward me, 'I think you've been so clever making it known that you want privacy. That's why, right now in this place, no-one dares come and ask for your autograph. Very clever of you.'

I looked at Lois in surprise, 'Well, er... I didn't consciously make any decision like that.' I looked cautiously around and saw that people were staring at me again.

'It's Melanie, her agent's idea.' Adam leant forward now and spoke quietly, 'She told me she was going for it... you know that sort of leave me alone type of celebrity always gets more attention. Like Emma Stone or Helen Bonham Carter. Back in history, Greta Garbo, I always annoy Eve by telling her she's an absolute ringer for the great Garbo. I don't suppose you know who she is... you're too young... unless you're into old movies.'

Lois sat up straight and nodded enthusiastically,

'Oh yes, she was so cool, and you're right, Eve does look incredibly like her. Same bone structure. I love the Thirties look.' She swept her long hair over one eye and said in a husky voice 'I just want to be alone!'

Toni and Adam both laughed, and I managed a weak smile as they launched into an animated conversation about the movies of the thirties. Apparently, Lois and Toni were both mad about old black and white films. I let the conversation drift on without me, while I thought about my Melanie, working away for me in London. How was it that she had spoken to Adam about her new strategy of marketing me as unapproachable? For a brief moment, I thought about standing up and asking out loud if anyone would like my autograph. But, of course, I didn't. Then I thought about being considered a likeness to the Great Garbo. I realised it was a compliment, but I resented the idea of being like anyone at all. The whole subject had come up when we had been in Frascati. Mistaken identities had caused us a great deal of trouble. No, it was no fun being a look-alike. I sipped my ice-cold lime and soda and studied the menu that Adam had placed in the middle of the small copper-coated table. It was quite enough of a problem to decide what to order. Starters and sharers? I would contemplate the meaning of the menu and worry about the meaning of life and double lives sometime later. Triple cooked chips? Now, why would that be? I decided to focus my attention back to the conversation. It had moved on, and Lois was now talking,

'I'm not at all sure we should do it, Toni. What do you think, Eve? Your father was a financial genius, wasn't he?'

That jolted me into awareness. Not only did I dislike talking about my absconding tycoon father, but I had no idea what it was that Lois and Toni should or should not do. 'Well, er... let me think for a moment.'

Adam kindly came to my rescue, probably guessing that I hadn't been concentrating. 'I don't think Eve's father believed in gambling on horses from what Bernard said the other day. Putting all your savings on a horse seems a fairly wild idea to me.' Adam looked at me across the top of his glass and raised his eyebrows. I gasped aloud,

'Putting your savings on a horse? Goodness, that sounds incredibly risky.'

Toni frowned and looked at Lois as he spoke to me. They seemed to need to stare into each other's eyes as they talked. It was rather disconcerting, but not nearly as worrying as Toni's scheme. He spoke earnestly, 'But it's an entirely sure thing. I had the tip only this morning. It's a chance to more than double our money. We could afford a deposit on our own flat and have a honeymoon.'

There was a quiet longing in his voice that made me feel even more worried for them. Still looking at each other, Lois replied,

'But we could lose everything we have saved, everything. Tell him, Eve. You're clever, and you know about money.' Her voice was loaded with anxiety. I had to say something,

'I know about losing money, that's for sure.' I was surprised at my own words. I rarely talked about my father, but I never ever talked about my own plummeting fall from wealth. I struggled to keep my voice calm as I continued, 'Is there any such thing as a sure thing?'

Our lunch in the pub, or rather our pub lunch, faltered on. I managed to avoid the subject of my father and his spectacular financial crash. Perhaps this was another reason why I shunned my ridiculous new TV fame. My father had fallen into infamy when he disappeared from the City of London. He had been highly esteemed all my life until the moment when his world collapsed around him... dragging me down in the slipstream. I knew very well that my new successful life was not just due to my knowledge of wine. There's a curious morbid delight that the general public has in watching catastrophe. I was a walking disaster, or rather I had escaped, seemingly unscathed, from financial ruin. I am sure many of my viewers were waiting for me to fall flat on my face. I looked around the small room of the pub again. People were all talking and laughing in groups and not paying me any attention now. I relaxed a little and nibbled a slice from the enormous hunk of cheese that I had ordered as a ploughman's lunch. Obviously, men that pushed a plough ate very well in Suffolk. I looked up at Adam and saw he was looking at me and smiling.

'That's a large piece of cheese for a Princess. Pass it over here when you've had your mouse-like nibble.'

I nodded and then decided to make another attempt at pub social skills.

'So, Toni, you must be very busy with the races coming up at the weekend. Do you work for one particular stable?'

'Oh yes, where I work there are over a hundred horses on a regular basis, so it's more than enough to keep me busy.' Toni managed to drag his eyes away from Lois for a moment and looked at me as he spoke. He did have the most beautiful, luminous dark brown eyes, fringed with inky, black lashes. Hmm, I thought it would be very hard to resist letting him put one's life savings on any horse he fancied. Then, returning to gaze at Lois he said,

'In fact, I have to get back to the stables by two.

Lois and me, we have a room over the stable. It comes with my job.'

Adam stood up and went over to the bar, and I guessed he was getting the bill. I guessed, too, that he thought, as I did, that Lois and Toni might want some time together in this room over the stables. I swallowed the last of my soda and said,

'We should be moving on, too. I'm visiting a vineyard this afternoon.'

'Do you have time to come to the stables?' Toni asked and looked as though he meant it. 'You might be interested in seeing the horses. Maybe Adam could take some photos?'

Lois looked at her mobile and pulled a face, 'I have a client at two thirty, so I can't come back with you. I'd better go straight back to the Royal Park. It's Sara Fellowes for a manicure. She says a manicure always makes her feel more confident when she has a cookery class. She's not really a trained chef or anything. She looks recipes up on Google.' Lois finished the last of her Caesar salad and then looked sadly at Toni, 'I won't see you until this evening, about six.'

I was wondering if and how I could possibly say anything to Lois about the need for her to be more discreet about her customers, but then Adam returned to the table,

'I'd love to see your stables and maybe watch you work? Could we manage an hour before we need to get to the Fellowes.' Adam looked at me and I nodded quickly, realising he was asking my permission. Before I could say anything, Lois said,

'Is it the Fellowes vineyard you're visiting? I hope you can write something lovely about them, Eve. It might be their saving.'

'Saving? In what way?' I asked, aware that Lois was about to divulge more about her client's private life and now curious to know more.

'Oh, they're always dodging bankruptcy.' Lois answered cheerily, 'Poor Sara, word is that her husband has a big gambling problem and her kids are just dreadful to her.'

'Really?' Now I was agog with the need for more gossip. 'But they seem to have such a perfect life.'

'Oh, that's Sara all over. She's such a lovely woman, but she never takes off her rose-tinted glasses. Last year they had to sell off a painting, Gainsborough or Constable or someone like that.'

'Well, that would certainly get them back on track.' I sighed, remembering my own small Paul Klee drawing that I had reluctantly sold.

'Oh yes, I think it went at auction for a small fortune but... well, money soon goes in that place. Their kids are constantly running into debt at uni, both of them. Sara just lets them off and pays up. She simply adores them and spoils them rotten. Same with her husband, I suppose. There she is working her socks off, running a cookery school on top of everything else she does. I think she only comes to the Spa to keep in with the rich people and sort of look rich herself.'

'Goodness.' I could think of nothing more to say and fortunately, at that point, Toni stood up and pulled Lois to her feet and silenced her with a swift but passionate kiss.

'She's a real beauty.' Adam gently stroked the soft nose of a bay horse that was pushing her head against the stable door. 'So, she's the one you're thinking of placing all your hard-earned money on then?'

Toni walked across the yard and stopped in surprise, 'Good God, I've never seen Miss Mopp looks so calm. You must have a way with her, Adam. Usually, she tries a mean snapping bite at anyone who cares to pass by her.'

Adam continued to stroke the horse's soft pinkish muzzle and rested his own forehead against hers. 'But you're a sweetie pie, Miss Mopp, don't listen to a word they say.'

Toni turned to me where I was standing at a safe distance from any possible biting range. To me, Miss Mopp looked a wild-eyed animal with a great deal of attitude. As soon as we had walked into the yard she had begun pushing her stable door and nosing at the door-bolt as though she knew how to unlatch it.

'Is Adam some sort of horse whisperer in his spare time, Eve? Honestly, I've never seen Miss Mopp behave so sweetly. I always have the devil of a job shoeing her. I need to check her shoes, now, but I've been putting it off all day. She's a beauty but, like all beautiful women, she likes her share of attention.'

Adam was now playing a gentle game of shaking his head at the horse and I smiled to see how Miss Mopp copied him.

'I know he does have a way with horses. I think he spent a good deal of time playing with gypsy lads and their ponies when he was a kid. I saw him ride when we were in Tuscany recently... he has... well, an unorthodox style.'

'Do you ride?' Toni asked as he began to sort out his various rasps and clippers from a leather bag.

'Oh yes, I rode a lot as a child... well, until quite recently really.' I stopped, unwilling to explain that I had recently had to sell my horse... nor did I want to say that I had played polo. It just sounded too... I found I was searching for the right word in my own head but could only come up with wealthy. Was there anything so wrong with having been wealthy? Standing now in a yard with so many horses, each worth a small fortune, the whole idea of money seemed ridiculous. I looked up at the sky and saw the clouds were gathering overhead. I decided rather than bother with my usual self-doubts or bitterness about my lost riches... I would, as I often did, adroitly change the subject.

'It looks as though you might get your rain this afternoon.'

Toni looked up at the pale blue Suffolk sky and the fluffy clouds blowing in from the east.

'Yep, the forecast is going to be right. The odds will change by tomorrow on our Miss Mopp. I'm not the only guy on the planet who knows she's a mudlark. Biggest hooves of any racehorse I've ever shod. I told Lois we had to place our bet as soon as possible.'

I seemed to have changed the subject to another problem. Surely, Toni would not persuade Lois to put all their savings on this horse? I looked again at Adam and Miss Mopp who was now chomping on a carrot. What was it that Bernard had said my father told him? Horse-racing is animated roulette? I reluctantly decided to make an attempt at some completely uneducated words of wisdom.

'Supposing you lose?' I said, wishing I could think of something or anything more to add.

Toni turned his back on me and went over to Adam, calling back over his shoulder, 'Miss Mopp is going to win on Saturday, I know it.'

As he drew near, Miss Mopp shook her head and made a passing snap of her big teeth at Toni. He easily dodged out the way and then laughed, 'See what I mean, Adam. She always does that to me.'

Adam continued to fondle the horse's ears, 'Ah, that's nothing, Toni, more of a love bite. As you said, she knows she a beauty and she's feisty with it.' Adam laughed and looked across to me, 'I love a woman with attitude.'

Then his face turned more serious, and he frowned, 'But how on earth you can risk all your money and Lois', too, on a horse to win... that's beyond me. I mean, she may be a beauty but just look round the yard. I can see at least four other nags that look fabulous.'

I followed Adam's hand as he waved a carrot to illustrate his point and and looked at several horses now poking their heads over their stable doors. Three of them bays and one chestnut. I said thoughtfully,

'I've often thought that horses do look alike until you get to know them. But I suppose they do all have distinctive markings.'

'Not to mention microchips.' Toni stroked the neck of the bay horse in the stable next to Miss Mopp. 'Couldn't be any racing without microchip identification.'

Adam looked at Toni with interest, 'Is that so? I read something about that once. I suppose it's like tagging.'

'The BHA and the Jockey Club here keep all the records. No chance of a dodgy ringer any more.'

'A ringer? Of course, that used to happen, didn't it.' Adam nodded, 'I remember at the Walthamstow stadium there was a huge fight over a greyhound ringer that was brought in.' Adam picked up the bits of carrot that Miss Mopp had dropped and fed her again from the flat of his hand. Toni laughed,

'I'd never have believed it if I hadn't seen it with my own eyes. Miss Mopp would have my thumb off if I offered her a bit of a carrot. If you ever want a career change, Adam, you should work in a stables.'

'I'd love to. Maybe when we've finished off this bloomin' wine book, I'll come and visit you for a few days and you can show me the tricks of your trade.'

'Really? Would you really do that? Why? You're a famous London photographer, aren't you?'

'Maybe, but there are a lot of things I'm longing to do when this book is wrapped up.' Suddenly Adam was staring at me, his eyes bluer than any Suffolk sky. I breathed in sharply and nodded at him and smiled as I said,

'Well, then, we'd better get over to the Fellowes' vineyards and finish off our work there. I agree, there are other things to do than work on this book.'

We thanked Toni for his time and wandered together out of the yard. We walked side by side, our hands almost touching... but not quite. I was happy with my thoughts of the future, but there was something that niggled at me. By the time we reached the car, I knew what it was. The word 'ringer' was clanging like a warning bell in my ears.

16

'You must be glad to be back in the driver's seat, Bernie. Well, you would be if you'd seen how the Princess treated your Merc. Parking in a bush and then she was drunk as a skunk at the pub. I had to pour her into the back seat to stop her from driving me back to the Royal Park.'

Bernard gave a sideways glance and frowned, 'Skunk... is drug, no?'

I gave one of my well-practiced sighs and wondered, as usual, whether or not to translate and decipher Adam's rhyming slang and joking lies. Then I saw that Bernard was already smiling,'

'Ah yes, *mais oui*, is the English humour, *n'est ce pas?*'

'Please don't think that Adam's idea of humour is typically English, Bernard. Anyway, just ignore him and tell me what happened at the hotel. Did you find the Ferrari men?'

'*Bien sur*, I find them, and I hear them, too.'

'You're a slippery eel, Bernie. For a big guy, you can make yourself disappear very quickly.'

'Now is talk of heels? Eve is right, Adam, I ignore you and, *bien sur*, I have training to be not seen. Is undercover work, is what I did in my old days in the police, *c'est normale*.'

'So, what did you hear, Bernard?' I leant forward from the back seat and put my head between the two men, not just to hear better, but to provide some sort of language barrier. This was another time not to sort out Adam's idiomatic English. We were well on our way to the Fellowes' vineyards and then there would be no more opportunity to talk until the evening. 'Was there anything said that was interesting?'

'They talk very long time about money and odds. I think was racing talk and difficult to understand. *Très difficile*.'

'I knew I should have gone back instead of you, Bernie. I would have understood everything.'

'Yes, but you would never have got near enough to hear them at all, Adam.' I spoke impatiently, 'How could a well-known photographer... a long-haired blonde six-footer in a Parka go un-noticed?'

'True.' Adam turned to me, and his face was very close to mine. His dark, blonde lashes framed and softened the blue of his eyes and he looked sweetly admonished. I had an almost irresistible desire to kiss him full on his mouth. Almost. Instead, I turned quickly to look at Bernard. His profile was stern and dark, and he looked quite unworried by Adam's accusation. He just looked calmly straight ahead as he continued,

'I understood everything that was important. Anyway, you can hear all later. I have recording, *bien sur*.'

'Recording?' Adam and I repeated the word together and I sat back in my seat again.

'*Bien sur, c'est normale.*'

'Bernie, my man, say not normal pa at all in my world. How did you manage that?'

'*Très facile*, is easy nowadays. My phone has memory enough. Nowadays everyone is paparazzi, photographer and a spy, *n'est ce pas?*'

'Maybe you're right, Bernard but, please, tell us now what you discovered.'

'The Irish, Mick Flanagan, he talks very much, his accent very strong. He is the confident one but is not so clever, I think. The other man, now I know is called Rupert, he is worried. He thinks there is big problem. He knows that you are TV celebrity and that Adam is famous photographer. On Saturday there is a race, and they know you are invited.'

Adam turned around to look at me, 'We are? Something you forgot to tell me, Princess?'

'That's because we haven't been invited.'

Bernard reached into the glove pocket and pulled out an envelope. He handed it back to me. 'This was left for you at reception. The girl asks me to give you.'

I took the envelope, a good quality, heavy cream envelope with my name hand-written in black ink on the front. I slit it open quickly and read the card inside.

'My mistake, it seems we are invited after all. This is from the secretary of the Jockey Club, requesting our attendance at the July races on Saturday. Lunch, at two, Premier Enclosure plus grandstand and paddock... your name is on it, too, Adam.' I passed the card forward, and Adam took it and read it through.

'Strict dress code, out with my best whistle then. But, how did this Mick and his mate Rupert know before we did?'

'I check out this Rupert already. He is Rupert Breville and a member at this club of jockey. I think is why he knows. But now he is very worried about... how you say, *l'intérêt médiatique, surtout en ce moment,* both of you... *faisant les gros titres... Eve, bien sur, tenant la vedette.'*

Adam looked at me, his eyebrows raised, 'Does that all mean what I think it means? You're a nuisance being there as you're a star?'

'You, too, Adam. You're headline news at the moment, especially since your exhibition at the Imperial War Museum. Yes, unfortunately, we're hitting the media headlines. Ridiculous and annoying.'

'Maybe so, just flavour of the minute, I guess. But why does it worry the Ferrari guys so much. They must be up to something dirty.'

'True, it's obvious they don't want the Press around if they're up to something underhand and devious.'

'Underhand and devious. How I love your language, Princess. It's even better than my slang. But do you expect Bernard to understand you? Shall I translate, Bernie?"

'Is OK, thank you, Adam, as you say, if it mean what I think then, yes, they are planning a crime. The question is... what?'

We were all silent for a minute or so, each thinking about the many possibilities of a crime at a race course. Adam spoke first,

'Well, it's obviously going to involve bad money or false betting... some complicated sort of cheating. It's really not my field of expertise, although I did mis-spend some of my youth at the dogs and there were all sorts of scams going on. Some great fights, too. But, of course, I was too young and sweetly innocent to be involved.'

Bernard laughed, 'Is hard to imagine you as innocent boy, Adam.'

'Well, maybe innocent is too strong a word, but I was trying to use English that you would understand, Bernie.'

'Hmm, *bien sur*, I see very well, Adam. But why you go to this dog-racing? You were a gambler?'

'Good God, no. I valued any bit of money I had as far too precious to risk on a skinny dog chasing a toy rabbit. No, I worked on a hot-dog stand and sometimes I groomed the dogs. I loved that.'

'Don't tell me you're a dog whisperer as well, Adam.' I sat forward again, 'Bernard, you should have seen Adam at the stables we visited after lunch. There was this big wild mare kicking up trouble and Adam just calmed her until they were practically kissing friends.'

'Isn't that rather idiomatic English, Eve? How do you expect Berie to understand all that. Kissing friends, indeed. Still, I'm not sure I can explain that now, sorry Bernie. But you know, I have a lot of experience of handling a stroppy high-bred mare.' Adam smoothed my hair as he spoke and I managed to give him a quick slap on the top of his head.

'*Non, non, mes enfants*, no fighting in my car. Please sit back, Mademoiselle Eve. Soon we are at the Fellowes' place and if you want to fight you can do so in the vineyards. Not, in my car.'

Bernard spoke very sternly and Adam, and I began to giggle. How often had it been on our travels that Bernard had made us feel like naughty children? But then

Bernard spoke again in a quieter voice, almost as though he was asking himself a question.

'But why is it these men, they talk always of the ring?'

Adam and I stopped laughing as quickly as we had begun and I clutched my hand to my cheeks in sudden realisation.

'Not a ring, Bernard. I know now, they must be talking about a ringer.'

17

'Yes, we expect a good year. The rain yesterday gave the grapes a good wash... no problems at the moment. They're ripening well.'

I was trying to concentrate on Hugo Fellowes' words as we walked along the top row of the vineyard. There had been no time at all to carry on our conversation in the car. The moment I had come to the realisation that the Ferrari men must be planning to substitute a horse in the Saturday races... at that very moment, we had arrived at the Fellowes' manor house. As soon as Bernard drew to a halt, a large black Labrador had dashed up to the car and Hugo Fellowes was there to greet us.

Now, as he escorted me through the rows of vines, I struggled to appear interested in his description of their wine production. Not only was my mind working through how we could expose the plot... or how we could prove it... or stop it... or... anything at all. Not only all these wild ideas were rushing through my head in confused disorder but what remained of the wine-writer's side of my brain was now filled with the idea that the charming Hugo was a compulsive gambler, running his hard-working wife, Sara, into the realm of bankruptcy. Bankruptcy was something I had recent knowledge of and I wouldn't wish it on my worst enemy.

So, I struggled to concentrate on the moment. Maybe a chapter in my book could help Sara stay solvent? There is no better publicity than free publicity. If I added my seal of approval to the Fellowes' wines and devoted the sixth chapter in my glossy book to their vineyard, then I knew it would bring them enormous sales. It was a ridiculous truism and as crazy as all the media interest in me at the moment. Adam deserved his stardom, and I understood why the general public would honour and respect him. He had earned his fame, bringing back his collection of sensitive and disturbing photographs from war-torn Afghanistan. I looked across to where Adam stood now, talking to Hugo Fellowes. How did Adam cope with the memory of the horror he had seen through his viewfinder? Was he finding recovery with this work, taking photos of the peaceful vineyards of France and Italy and now here in Suffolk? How did he manage to be so constantly upbeat and humorous? I looked up at a small flock of birds wheeling in the sky above our heads. Clouds were forming in a dark mass and the afternoon seemed to be turning early to the dusk of evening. There were no answers written across the sky and I made a conscious effort to straighten my shoulders and get back to the work on hand. Work was always my solution.

'Your vines are beautifully tended... how many people do you employ?'

'Well, we have five full-time staff and then, of course, we employ more for the harvest. Then I have two permanent lab workers. Would you like to see my lab?'

I thought for a moment that Hugo was talking about his black Labrador. The dog had accompanied us on our inspection of the vines, and I had seen quite enough of him as he jumped around, splattering me with mud. Just in time, I realised that Hugo was offering to show me his laboratory. Hugo, the brilliant biochemist, according to his devoted wife.

'Yes, that would be interesting.' I smiled and dodged another playful leap from the Labrador. It was beginning to rain, and the thought of a clean, warm laboratory held a certain appeal.

We walked quickly back toward the manor, Hugo striding ahead of us, his head down as the light drizzle became a downpour. I pulled my Burberry around me and Adam, his Parka hood over his head, put his arm over my shoulders.

'Do you want my Parka, Eve?'

'No, I'm fine, thanks.' The thought of sheltering in the voluminous folds of his Parka was very tempting, but just his arm around my shoulders was enough. Once again, even in the damp Suffolk air, I could pick up the scent that was so essentially Adam. I breathed in gently and wondered if I would ever be able to define it. We hurried on and I tried to concentrate on the work ahead. Certainly, the vineyards were well organised and maintained and the scenery, even now in the gloom of late afternoon, was beautiful in a quintessentially English way. The gentle landscape of Constable or Gainsborough stretched out before us, pale mist gathering around the distant clumps of oak forests, dark against the leaden sky. How would Adam be able to capture and conjure up the magic of the land? But then, he was some sort of magician. I smiled to myself at the thought and, even though it must have been absolutely impossible for him to see my face, Adam said quietly,

'What are you smiling about now, Princess?'

'If you really want to know... er, I was thinking you're a magician.'

Adam laughed and gave me a small squeeze, 'I wish. I'd cast you in my spell as quick as you can say abracadabra.'

I made no reply as we had arrived at the door of a large timber barn and Hugo was holding it open for us. I went in quickly and then stopped in surprise. The ancient barn had been converted into a high-tech laboratory. Not even at some of the largest vineyards in France had I seen anything like it. I blinked at the unexpected white brightness, and my first thought was that is must have cost a small fortune to set up. Hugo closed the door firmly, leaving the black Labrador outside the very white laboratory and turned to me, his face alight with enthusiasm.

'I can see you're surprised, Eve. This is the new age of wine.'

'Indeed, I'm amazed. You are certainly very well equipped for a small wine producer, but then, of course, you are a biochemist, aren't you. I remember Sara mentioning it.'

'Yes, yes.' Hugo answered vaguely as he was already examining some statistics on one of the computer screens. The two young women working at a long steel counter came over to talk with him, and I left them to it.

Adam was already busy taking photos, obviously enjoying the reflections in the steel vats and glass phials. I didn't want to tell him that any photo he took in here would not appear in a book of mine. This was not what my readers would want. My approach to wine was much more organic. I almost shuddered in the cold, sterile air of the laboratory. The chemistry of oenology and viticulture was becoming more sophisticated and technical year by year. Quality control, health and safety standards, processing by analytical procedures... all the giant ogres of the wine world. I smiled then, as I remembered a sunny day in Tuscany, one of our earlier assignments, standing beside a wine grower who chose when to begin his harvest by biting a grape and testing the thickness of the skin and the size of the seeds inside. It seemed a million years away from where I stood now, watching Hugo, his face lit by the blue-white light of a computer screen.

Adam had finished taking his photos and wandered outside. As he went through the door, I saw him bend and stroke the rain-soaked black Labrador waiting outside. Then the door closed, and with the slight sound, it made, Hugo turned around. He seemed to suddenly remember that I was there. He began to explain the work of his laboratory, his face now alight with an internal fanaticism. I listened and listened... and listened. It was nearly an hour later when I finally made my escape from the cold white lab.

18

'You must be longing for a cup of tea. Let me take your wet coat.' Sara Fellowes rushed toward me, her arms wide in welcome. Hugo had pointed out the cookery school barn across the yard from his laboratory. He had offered to accompany me, but I had been glad to escape, and he seemed very pleased to stay in his laboratory.

The converted barn, where Sara held her cookery classes, was quite the opposite to Hugo's shiny white and clinical laboratory. Here, the air was warm and filled with the smell of good cooking and I breathed in appreciatively. Large amber glass lights hung down from the high vaulted ceiling, casting pools of bright light over six refectory tables and I saw Adam, happily ensconced at one of the scrubbed wood tables, scoffing cake and chatting with a group of women.

I smiled gratefully at Sara, 'Yes, that would be lovely, it's certainly good to be in the warm. The weather has turned quite cold.'

'I hope Hugo hasn't been boring you for too long in his lab.' Sara smiled brightly, but there were well-etched lines of anxiety around her face.

'Goodness, no, not at all. It was all most interesting. You have a very sophisticated laboratory for the size of your vineyard.'

'Earl Grey, Lapsang, Builders... anything you like?'

'Earl Grey would be lovely, thank you.' I realised that Sara was not going to continue any further into talk about the laboratory. I think she knew, and even guessed that I knew, that it was just a very expensive boy-toy room for Hugo to play in. My heart went out to the woman as I watched her dash over to the Aga and lift a heavy kettle to brew my tea. There was something desperate in her every effort to make life cosy and rosy. Lois had said that Sara wore rose-tinted glasses, but I admired Sara's strength and loyalty. Adam raised a hand in greeting and stood up.

'Come and join the tea party, Eve. Let me introduce you to these ladies who lunch... and that's after they've had coffee and before they take cream tea.'

There was general laughter amongst the group and one spoke up.

'That's not all we do, Adam. You only met us after we had our aqua gym class. We exercise like mad and then we can enjoy our wicked sins.' She stood up, a tall, elegant woman dressed in classic style, and held out a be-ringed hand to me. 'Delighted to meet you, Eve, we are all great fans of yours.'

There was a great commotion, then, as they all stood up to make room for another chair at the table. One by one, they introduced themselves and I realised that it was the same women I had seen earlier on the terrace of the Royal Park. Sara brought over a tray of tea for me. I sat down and felt more relaxed than I had all day. It was warm, the women were convivial and not asking awkward questions... and there was cake.

Sara cut me a slice and said, 'Will you give me your honest opinion of this yoghurt cake. We've been making lavender-perfumed biscuits this afternoon, but this is a cake I made earlier.'

'Thank you, it looks fantastic.' I took a small bite and saw that everyone was watching me, awaiting my verdict. I was very accustomed to wine-tasting and being tested and sometimes tricked. This was a piece of cake in comparison.

'Mmm, delicious, light and airy but just moist enough.' I took another bite and then smiled around at them. 'But if you really want to know then...' I took another small bite and looked around at the waiting faces, 'I should say, after the obvious background flavour of the batter made with fresh eggs and good white flour, mmm, I should say the bacterial fermentation of the milk... the tangy yogurty taste is prevalent, probably a thick curdled and strained Greek yoghurt. But it is almost masked, or rather enhanced by the honey, very perfumed, possibly acacia and then there is a touch of vanilla... probably in the sugar?' I ended abruptly and with a polite inferred question mark, although I was very sure of my analysis. I took another bite and was delighted to receive a round of applause. Adam took his seat again and beamed at everyone.

'Isn't she simply amazing? I mean to me, the cake is scrummy, and that's it.'

There was some laughter and then one of the women, a sweet-faced woman with turquoise blue eyes and silvery gold hair said, quite out of the blue, 'I think it's so wonderful that you two should meet.'

Everyone turned to her, waiting for her to continue, but she just took another drink of her tea and remained silent. Another woman, strong-faced and with steely well-cut grey hair and a determined slant to her perfectly plucked eyebrows spoke up,

'Go on, Suzanne, you always do that. You say something seemingly quite irrelevant and then stop. Tell us, what did you mean?'

'What did I mean?' The woman called Suzanne looked up to the beamed ceiling, her startling blue eyes searching, 'Adam meeting Eve, it's so biblical.'

Now there was a silence and then some laughter. It wasn't as though I hadn't thought about it myself. When we had first met in that marble-floored hotel in Haute-Savoie, when Adam had walked into my orderly five-star life in his snow-laden Parka... yes, of course, we had laughed at the combination of our names. Somehow, since then, it had become quite every day. I looked at Adam and found that he was looking at me. I had the uncanny feeling that he was thinking about that first moment, too. Then he spoke,

'You're quite right, Suzanne, it does have a biblical resonance. When I first met Eve, on an ice cold night in the high mountains of Courchevel... how I remember that moment. Eve was standing in the centre of the lobby of the grandest of hotels. Somehow she managed to look as though she owned it and yet, yes... there was a fragility there, too. I wanted to be near her and look after her from that moment on. Then I stupidly said something about an apple.'

The women were all leaning toward Adam, as though magnetised by every word of his story. I thought about how I had called him a magician... and he was, surely?

19

Back in the car, it all suddenly came rushing back to me.

'What are we going to do about the Ferrari men?'

Adam was sitting, as he often did, in the front passenger seat beside Bernard. Neither of the men answered straight away, and I carried on, speaking my worried thoughts aloud. Problems that had been pushed to the back of my mind all afternoon, 'I mean, do you really think they're planning on a ringer?'

Bernard nodded slowly, 'While you are at the Fellowes', I have been thinking about it all. I phoned again my friend in the Met. He said is impossible. All racehorses are microchipped and tested and checked again just before the race. There were many times in the past... these ringers, but no, now he says is impossible.'

'He should know, I suppose,' Adam said doubtfully, ' but it does add up in some ways. I mean, if the Ferrari guys could somehow arrange a swap of horses and bet themselves on a dead cert... well, I don't know anything about it really, but it sort of makes sense.'

'I know even less than that, but I just don't get the idea that they would be talking about my ring, or any ring. The whole thing is driving me mad.'

Bernard sighed, 'Is true, it is not possible is about your ring, Mademoiselle Eve. That was a stupid idea. Why would they think it impossible now that you are here in Newmarket. No, it would be the reverse, *n'est ce pas*? How could they plan to steal your ring, even if they thought you still owned it... I mean how could they plan it if you were not here. No, is ridiculous.'

There was a silence in the car now, as we all thought about it. Then Adam slapped his hand on his knee in exasperation. 'Why don't I just go up to them as soon as we see them again and ask them just what the hell they're up to?'

'What you think they say, Adam?' Bernard shook his head, and I saw him frown as he glanced sideways at

Adam, ' I understand is natural to think like that for you, but is not a solution. When we get back to the Royal Park, I like you both to listen to my recordings. Maybe you hear something I not understanded.'

'Good idea, Bernard. At least that is something practical we can do.'

There was another silence as Bernard drove on, the rain beating now against the windscreen and the sky a solid flannel of grey. My thoughts returned to the Fellowes'. It had been a pleasant enough afternoon, but I knew there was something I had to say.

'Skipping from one problem to the next. I'm afraid that the Fellowes' vineyard doesn't really make an interesting story.'

Adam swivelled around in his seat and looked at me in dismay,

'You are joking, Eve? We've spent a good amount of time there and I've hundreds of shots. What the hell?'

'Sorry, I know but...'

'Don't worry about the photos I took in the lab. I knew you wouldn't be interested in any of them. I just took a few for my own interest. There were some interesting challenges in all the reflected glass and steel. I didn't dream you'd want them for your posh dreamy wine book. But, I'll show you the vineyard shots later. There are some really good, Constably Gainsboroughish landscapes... if that doesn't sound too conceited.'

'Oh please, don't let me stop you from being conceited, Adam.' I laughed and he turned round again to look through the windscreen. I could tell just by the set of his square shoulders under his Parka that he was very put out. I carried on, 'I thought I could use the cookery school as a point of interest. I think Sara does a great job at it and the guests were all so charming. What a lovely group of women.'

'There you are. That would make a great story. Lady of the manor, Sara Fellowes' opens her doors to welcome local ladies and cooks up a storm etc. etc.. You could do it so well. Come on, Princess, give me a break.

Say you'll change your mind and write it up and finish off the sixth chapter. Please.'

Now he turned back to me again, and he pulled a most beautiful Jesus face at me. But I shook my head at him,

'It's no good, Adam... the problem is that the wine is no good. No good at all. Everything I tasted, different years and different labels... well, they all tasted much the same... bland and dull. Sorry, but it's not going to happen. We'll have to find another vineyard.'

20

The recording ended with a quiet click and Adam, and I looked at each other. We were in my suite at the Royal Park, Bernard's mobile was on the table between us, still glowing. Bernard had his back to us as he stood by the long windows onto the terrace. It wasn't yet seven in the evening but the dark afternoon had slipped early into a moonless night.

'It seems quite clear to me, well, not completely clear maybe, but...'Adam shrugged his shoulders and stood up and joined Bernard at the window. 'You did a great job, Bernie, great job. The recording is clear enough but...'

I stood up, too, and stretched, 'But it is ambiguous.'

'Now isn't that just the most Princessy word for it. Am-big-you-us. Perfect. I always say you're so sexy when you talk posh, Princess.'

Bernard turned round suddenly, 'Now don't you two start one of your fights. This is not the time. Tell me, do you think they are planning to substitute a horse?'

Adam and I looked at each other and said at the same moment, 'Not sure.'

Bernard went to the table and snatched up his phone with a rare show of impatience. '*C'est vrai*, nothing to prove anything. If I send this to my friend in the Met he say same thing. No real evidence.'

I went to the wall switches and turned on the lights. The room was softly lit by three large table lamps. I pulled the curtains, hoping to exclude the dreary darkness and the problems.

'I think we should go down to dinner, we always think better after food. Especially you, Adam.'

'I have to say I am starving. That cake seems like a distant sweet memory. How about we go back to my idea of just confronting the Ferrari men? You know, call their bluff.'

Bernard and I, now, spoke together just one word, 'No.' and then Bernard added. 'Maybe they will be in restaurant, but we can say nothing, ask nothing. Is crazy idea.'

'I absolutely agree. We can't possibly confront them, Adam. We have no proof of anything except an arguably shady conversation about horses... and we illegally recorded them. We've probably broken some sort of privacy law. No, but we do need dinner. Come on.'

Less than half an hour later we were sipping soup, a very good creamy Vichysoisse, comforting enough, but it did little to improve our spirits. The dining room was full of guests, mostly eating and drinking too much, the excitement of the next day's races already in the air.

There was the usual embarrassing stir and a momentary pause in the general buzz of noise as I walked in. I switched on my TV star smile and quickly sat at our table without making direct eye contact with anyone.

The bar was busy popping Champagne corks, and I looked with interest at a Jeroboam that had been opened at one table and was being carefully poured. It seemed that life at the Royal Park was a very wealthy affair indeed.

I thought about the last time I had seen a Jeroboam of Champagne. It had been on my twenty-first birthday, a large formal party that my father had arranged. Everyone I knew seemed to be there, even my mother. She had made a late and dramatic entrance, dressed in dark scarlet taffeta, a sparkling necklace of rubies around her tanned neck and her latest husband on her arm. I smiled at the memory. There was nothing else to do. I could have been shocked by her arriving with a husband that I had never met. A good-looking young man who appeared to enjoy golf, surfing... and money. Yes, I smiled because it was possibly a perfect match and what was the point in harbouring resentment. I had been so young when she had deserted me that I hardly knew this vibrant woman in red silk. I was even relieved that she had taken the limelight that night. Taken credit, too, for my early success up at Cambridge. The Champagne had continued to pour until midnight when I cut my cake and made my wish. Did anyone there know that I wished to be away from the celebrations and on my own with a good book? Smiling, smiling until my face had ached with the effort. I have the photos to prove it. I saw, in my mind's eye one particular photo of me, knife raised above the cake, my father on my right and my mother, one long elegant arm around me, on my left. I had looked trapped, and my smile stretched to a rictus over the menace of the knife blade.

The numerous photos that Adam had taken of me over the last few months together, were so different. Whether it was his skill or because I was truly relaxed now... for whatever reason I looked strangely younger than all the formal photos taken in my past. I came back to the present moment and realised I was staring at Adam. He hadn't noticed because he was looking at Bernard, his face flushed and his hands gripping the edge of the white tablecloth. Then he turned to me,

'The Ferrari guys have just arrived.'

I stared down at my plate, trying to resist the desire to look around the room, my heart beginning to beat fast in my chest. 'Where are they sitting, Adam? Can I look?'

'They're at a table near the door we came in by, directly behind you. No, don't turn round now, they're looking this way.'

Bernard looked at me across the table. 'I see them from here, but there is nothing we can do. Nothing. Now, the concierge is talking to them.'

'David? The concierge, is he here in the restaurant?' I could hardly bear not to turn around.

'He just came in and seems to be making a stop at a few tables. He's coming this way now.

At last, I turned slightly as David now stopped at our table. I flashed another TV smile at him,

'Good evening, David. How are you?' He bent slightly towards us, a tall elegant man who fitted perfectly into the luxury surroundings of the hotel.

'I'm very well, Miss Sinclair, thank you for asking. I hope you are enjoying your stay here at the Royal Park.'

'Oh yes, everything in simply perfect.' David nodded his head in satisfaction and was about to move on when I added, after another of my best professionally radiant smiles, 'Except for one thing, actually.'

David stood upright and held his hand over the top pocket of his jacket as though I had shot him through the heart. 'Something is wrong?' His face was creased with concern. 'Please tell me, I am sure I can sort out any problem you may have.'

I indicated the empty chair beside me, 'Won't you join us for a moment. I would like a word with you, if you have time.'

David sat down quickly, unbuttoning his immaculate jacket and smoothing the crease in his trousers. He looked worried and so I went straight to the point.

'Nothing really to do with the hotel. It seems to me that the Royal Park runs perfectly smoothly. But I wonder if I could take you into my confidence?' I leant toward him slightly, and glanced quickly at Bernard and then Adam. They both nodded quickly, and I knew they had guessed the direction I was heading. 'You see, David, I'm trying to get used to my new celebrity status but I find it very difficult sometimes. Just the other day I overheard two of your clients talking about me and, well, the drift of their conversation made me feel rather frightened.'

As I spoke, David had at first relaxed, happy that his realm of the Royal Park was not at fault. Then as I continued he looked mystified as he replied,

'Two clients?'

'Actually, they are in rooms on my floor, numbers twenty-two and twenty-three.'

'I see, well, if there is anything I can do... but I don't quite understand.'

'Oh, I completely understand that you have to protect the privacy of all your clients but, well, you see... I overheard that they are planning to steal a very valuable ring that my father gave me, a diamond ring.'

David drew in his breath sharply, 'Well, in the circumstances, I can tell you that they are Mick Flanagan and Rupert Breville, neither have stayed with us before. I shall certainly keep my eye on them and report back anything I find out. As for your ring, shouldn't you put it in the hotel safe immediately.'

'Absolutely, I have it in my bag now, and I'll go to reception straight after dinner.' I smiled again, as though he had now solved my problem,'Will you take a coffee now?'

David still looked very concerned, 'Thank you, Miss Sinclair, but I think I should go straight away and see to this problem.'

'Why thank you, David. Do call me Eve, and have you met my chauffeur, Bernard Guillaume? I was just wondering if he could help you in any way. He was once highly ranked in the French police. He likes to keep an eye on my security. If he could be of any help at all?'

Bernard leaned forward and offered his hand to David, saying, '*Enchanté, Monsieur*. You have a wonderful hotel here. I have seen many hotels all over Europe, working for the Sinclair family. I think the Royal Park is very fine.'

'Thank you, thank you. That is a great compliment. coming from someone who has worked for Robert Sinclair. Well, you must be quite an expert in protection then. I would be most grateful if you would help, of course. Miss Sinclair's safety is of utmost importance.'

'I think there is risk, *bien sur*.'

'You do?' David now looked very worried indeed. 'What do you suggest?' He looked at me as he spoke and I answered firmly,

'Perhaps you and Bernard could search their rooms while they are here at dinner?'

21

Adam and I sat a long time over coffee. David West had, at first, looked shocked at Bernard's quiet request to search the Ferrari guys' rooms but had suddenly nodded in agreement. He had moved away from our table and stopped briefly to chat with guests at a couple of other tables, before strolling casually out of the dining room. I watched him go and thought that my first impression of him had been right. He was a very cool character indeed. Bernard had a quick coffee and then left us, too. He went in the other direction as though heading for the car park. Adam and I were left sitting with our coffees, and very aware that we had to keep watch over the Ferrari men. Adam leant toward me and whispered in my ear.

'This is my chance to be up close and very romantic. Shame I have to watch the sleazy Mick and Rupe over your right shoulder.'

I put my lips close to Adam's ear and whispered back, trying hard to ignore the light perfume that always hung around him.

'What shall we do if they decide to leave and go back to their rooms?' I drew away from him, 'And this is absolutely no time to mess around, Adam.'

'I know that, Princess. I just said it was a shame, that's all. I thought we could go into a clinch, you know, like in the old movies when they want to pretend...' Adam saw that I was glaring at him angrily and he faltered to a stop as I interrupted him,

'And goodness knows what the press would make of us sitting so close together. It will be all over the papers tomorrow that we're what they call an item.'

'True enough. I recognise a guy from the Daily Mail over in the corner. Probably here for the races, but a romance story on you would make his day. I can see the headlines, Vinous Venus kisses upstart photographer.'

'Adam, stop it.' I managed an effective sharp kick on his shin while I picked up the menu.

'Ouch, you're so sneaky and cruel, Princess, but s'alright... only teasing you. I have a clear view of their table, if I peer under your delightful right ear lobe. Anyway, they haven't even ordered a dessert yet. The waiter has just taken away those huge wooden platters. They look like steak and chips guys. I bet they go for a black forest gateau or something and then probably Irish coffees. I think Bernie and your man, David, should have plenty of time for a quick shifty. I must say you manipulated that very well, your royal highness. You're not only a vicious kicker but you're a very sly Princess.'

'I wish I could turn round and see the Ferrari men for myself. Are you sure they're going to order desserts? Please, do I have to tell you again, take this seriously, Adam.'

'I am, I promise, and it's a dead cert they'll order puddings. They both look like big boozy eaters. So, whatever made you think of searching their rooms and then talking David West into it?'

'I don't know. I just suggested it on the spur of the moment. David has such a calm, capable manner, and I thought we could rely on him implicitly. Also, I was so fed up with not knowing anything. On top of all that, I was worried you'd suddenly jump up and confront the Ferrari men.'

'Funny you should say that Eve. The Irishman has just damned well signed the chitty. I misjudged them, they're not going for pud, so I'm going to jump up right now. Wait here a minute.'

To my surprise and dismay, Adam now did jump up from our table and went over to where the Ferrari men were sitting. I should have known there was no such thing as a dead cert. I turned around quickly, and saw that Adam was chatting to them, leaning over their table, but already the Irishman had begun to stand up. They were about to leave the dining room. My stomach butterflied in a moment of panic as I imagined them heading straight back to their rooms. I stood up quickly and went over to join

Adam. The men all turned to look at me as I drew near, and I smiled, my best professional smile.

'Good evening, we met the other night, didn't we. Have you been at the races today?'

'I was just saying to Mick, here, that we were going to the bar for a brandy. I thought perhaps they'd join us.' Adam raised his eyebrows at me and I hurriedly carried on where he had left off.

'Great idea. Let's go!' I actually slipped my hand through the arm of the man called Rupert and laughed with what I hoped was gaiety. The two men looked surprised and somewhat wrong-footed, but they moved along with us out of the dining room and into the bar.

Adam called to the barmaid and then turned to the men. 'What do you say we have a bottle of bubbly. I had some luck on the horses today.'

This seemed to strike a note that Mick recognised. 'Did you back the filly, Easy Rider? Did you? I wish I'd had that one.'

Adam was too wily to be tricked into an error, and he just touched the side of his nose and said, 'I never talk about the women or the horses in my life. It's a strict rule of mine.' Both the Ferrari men now laughed and seemed more at ease, although I felt completely out of place. The barmaid, a pretty girl with her hair drawn back in a tight plait, brought over a bottle of chilled Champagne and showed it to Adam.

'Good God, it's no use showing it to me, young lady.' Adam smiled at the girl and she flushed a delicate pink. 'Please show it to the expert sitting beside me in pale blue silk.'

The barmaid turned the bottle to show me the label, and I shook my head, 'No, I don't think so, do you have any Louis Roederer Cristal?'

'Certainly, certainly, an excellent choice.' The girl gave me a nervous smile and hurried away, her plaits bobbing, and soon returned with another bottle which again she showed to me. I nodded, and she began to carefully twist the wire. As the cork popped, I closed my eyes for a moment wondering how on earth we had got to this moment. How could we be sitting in a bar with these dreadful men and drinking fine Champagne? I couldn't really blame Adam as it had been a good plan to delay the Ferrari men but then he had been so wrong about them ordering desserts. Dead cert, indeed. I was struggling to remain calm, feeling both angry and scared in equal measures. There had been no time to even think about going to warn Bernard and David. The whole evening was rapidly becoming a fiasco. The young barmaid filled my glass, and the three men watched me closely as I took my first sip. The dry toasty fruitiness of the wine filled me with the usual pleasure that this elegant Champagne reliably delivered, and it gave me a little courage. All Adam and I had to do was to occupy these men for half an hour or so... how difficult could that be with such a wine to drink? I could probably spend at least fifteen minutes describing it. I raised my glass and resumed my unpracticed flirty, social butterfly behaviour.

'Your health, gentleman and I hope you have good luck at the races.'

The Irishman tipped the entire glass of his Champagne down his neck and held out his glass again.

'That's a fine drink, Miss Sinclair, a fine drink but these little glasses only wet my whistle.'

Adam hastily took the bottle from the ice bucket and carefully poured him another glassful. 'You have a thirst, Mick tonight then. Have you had a bad day?'

'Not so good, not so good to be sure. Jaysus, me heart went crossways in the last race.'

I sipped my wine and would have crossed my fingers if I could, in the hope that Adam had any idea how to carry on this conversation. Heart went crossways? What was that all about? Then, Rupert, the oily-voiced Londoner turned to talk to me directly,

'I suppose you drank this every day, before your father came to such a colossal cropper and threw half of London down into the mire.'

I was caught off my guard and felt my cheeks begin to burn with anger and some residual shame. I suspected, or dreaded, that Rupert might himself have lost money due to my father. Had he been an investor? The problem was that I had no idea how the whole financial crisis had come about. I had never taken the slightest interest in my father's world, and when it collapsed, I was as bewildered and bereft as anyone else. I took a deep breath and remembered what Adam had said before. Hadn't he admired the way I refused to be bullied and how I had taken charge of the conversation. I had to do the same again. I shook my long hair back and straightened my shoulders.

'Oh yes, we drank it every day at breakfast since I was about fifteen years old. Do you like Roederer or do you prefer another Champagne?'

Rupert looked taken aback and then he smiled, more of a grimace than a smile, showing all his teeth in a way that I knew revealed aggression. This man was truly monstrous. He continued,

'I see you've inherited your father's spirit, young lady. The Roederer is very good, but then you would only drink the best. How would you describe it?'

I gave a small sigh of relief as now I could spin out a long description and ward off any more of his spiteful taunts.

I took another small sip, 'Ah well, the Cristal is a great wine, created in 1876 to meet the demanding tastes of Tsar Alexander II. Not only the best cuvée but he also insisted on the distinctive transparent lead crystal, flat-bottomed bottle. Clear glass, so that any poison could be detected and a flat base so that nothing lethal could be hidden in the usual punt. Well, he had plenty of reason to fear assassination, as I'm sure you know.' I laughed merrily but gave no time for a reply. It was a technique I had often adopted at Cambridge, when I wanted to hold the floor at a seminar. So, I gushed on relentlessly, 'The Cristal is only produced in the best years when the grapes, approximately forty percent Chardonnay and sixty percent Pinot Noir, mature to perfection. Then, Cristal is always aged for six years in their cellars before they wait another eight months after *dégorgement*. The cellar master, Jean-Baptiste Lécaillon, is a complete genius, naturally. That's why it's a wine that can keep for twenty years or more without losing its wonderful fresh character.'

I took another very small sip and was amused to see that Rupert was almost squirming with impatience as he listened to my long drawn out description. But, I was by no means finished yet and before he could interrupt me, again, I continued,

'Mmm, remarkably balanced and refined with an amazing lengthy finish. So distinctive with its silky texture and light fruity aroma... and then a strong mineral quality... yes, delicious white fruit and clear citrus notes. Cristal is a wine that keeps well... er, as I said, it can be conserved for over twenty years without losing its freshness and character. It's complicated... serious, even, but the gravitas is lightened by sheer flamboyant pleasure. It's strange to think that it's so famous that it's drunk by people throwing their money around just for the name. Hip-hop and rap artists, film-stars and all sorts of general riffraff.'

I ended abruptly and took another sip from my glass. That should shut him up, I thought to myself. But it didn't. He had another idea up his sleeve and turned to the barmaid and muttered something that I couldn't hear.

Adam was still talking to Mick about racing, and I felt my ears beginning to sing with nerves. Then the barmaid brought out another ice bucket holding a bottle wrapped in a white linen napkin.

Rupert gave me another toothy leer and told the barmaid to open the bottle. I knew immediately that I was going to be asked to identify the wine. I sighed with exasperation and then felt relieved that at least is would take up a bit more time. Adam had now noticed the new bottle, and I think he guessed the game about to be played

Rupert passed me a glass of the new wine, his podgy fingers wrapped around the rim of the glass. I pulled a face of real disgust and the girl behind the bar, clearly another well-trained member of the staff at the Royal Park, quickly poured me another glass and handed it to me, holding it carefully by the stem. I took the glass and looked at it with interest. It had the colour of a good Champagne and the very fine bubbles were spiralling up the glass flute just as they should. Then Adam spoke up,

'If you're about to ask Eve to identify a wine, shall we make it more interesting. I'm happy to put some money on her being able to guess the grapes that made up this bubbly. What do you say, Mick? Will you put a monkey against Eve, at evens?'

'Guessing the grape, what are you on, boy? Isn't there a whole number of different grapes around the world. Well, that's what I thought. Sure, I'll put a monkey at evens.'

I looked at Adam in dismay, had he drunk too much Champagne? I knew he hardly ever drank alcohol, so perhaps the famous Roederer bubbles were leading him astray. I wasn't at all sure, but I had the idea that a monkey was what I would call five hundred pounds. I looked again at the sparkling glass in front of me. Probably, well, almost certainly, I would be able to tell the variety of the grapes, but it was not what I was beginning to know as a dead cert.

Then Rupert, still sneering, said,

'I don't think the pretty rich lady could ever guess the grape. I'll take your bet as well, Adam. I think she's just clever on TV, when it's all set up for her.'

Well, that decided me, '*Faites vo jeux*, gentlemen, place your bets.' I placed the glass upright under my nose and breathed in gently. Oh, this was going to be so easy. The men were still talking and Adam was actually writing down their bets on the back of the bar menu. Did they think I was a racehorse? But the time was passing swiftly and very soon, surely, we could safely let them go to their rooms. I swirled the wine gently in the glass and took in another breath. I saw they were all looking at me as I took my first sip. I blinked. Well, that was a surprise indeed. I let the wine roll over my tongue and enjoyed the cold mouthfeel on my palate... but I knew immediately that it was not Champagne. I looked at Adam and smiled, I knew he had just won his bets. The wine was very simple to identify although I was quite puzzled by its provenance. Fortunately, the bet was only to define the grape varieties. I took another sip and swallowed slowly, then spoke quietly but with confidence,

'Well, this is a very good quality sparkling wine, not Champagne, but made by the *méthode champenoise*. Soft and fruity in flavour...'

'Yes, yes, to be sure,' Mick interrupted me, 'That's all very fine and fancy. Now don't be starting with another of your long lectures. The grapes? I'm thinking you don't know the grapes. Am I right?'

'The grapes, good heavens, it's so obvious. You couldn't have given me an easier task after drinking the Roederer. Same grapes, you see. Ridiculously easy to identify.... Pinot Noir and Chardonnay, of course, anyone would know that at the first sniff.'

I gave the Irishman a steely glare and in response he slammed his delicate flute of wine on the table and smashed the stem. I ignored him and turned to Rupert, smiling and baring as many of my teeth as I could. 'Why don't you take the napkin off the bottle and read the back label?'

Rupert snatched the napkin up in his hand and threw it on the floor, sprinkling us all with icy water ashe read the back label.

'Temper, temper, Rupe!' Adam laughed and dabbed my arm with a paper napkin from the bar, 'No need to be a bad loser. I can afford to wait for my money if you're pushed.'

I thought perhaps Adam had gone too far in antagonising the men, and I decided to try and defuse the situation. I took the bottle from the bucket and looked at the front label. I drew in my breath in surprise. It came from the Fellowes' winery. Why had they never offered me their sparkling wine to taste? I was so shocked that I turned to Rupert and spoke the complete truth.

'You have no idea how you have solved a problem that I have been wrestling with all day.'

All three men looked at me in puzzlement, but at that moment I saw Bernard passing the doorway of the bar.

'Goodness, there's Bernard already. Sorry, gentlemen, you'll have to excuse us. I have a late meeting. We must dash. Come on Adam. We'll leave you with the rest of the bottle, gentleman, enjoy!'

22

'Will you stop, just for one minute, talking about wine?' Adam and I were hurrying back from the bar toward the hotel lobby.

'But, you don't understand, Adam. The sparkling wine was from the Fellowes' vineyard and it's extraordinarily good. In fact, it's a perfect young racy wine that...'

Adam took two paces ahead of me and turned round, walking backwards as he spoke, 'I don't care about the wine, stop, Eve, just stop. Have you forgotten we need to find Bernard?'

I looked at him vaguely as he hopped along backwards in front of me,

'Of course, I haven't,' I lied easily, as in truth I had put the matter of searching the rooms to the back of my mind. I was so delighted to find that I had discovered a good reason to write my chapter on the Fellowes'. The wine I had just tasted was possibly the best English sparkling wine I had ever come across. Then, as we reached the lobby, I saw Bernard waiting for us. 'Anyway, calm down, Adam. Bernard's waiting just over there.'

Adam turned around and went quickly to meet Bernard. I followed more slowly, somehow reluctant to get back to the whole murky business of what the Ferrari men were up to in Newmarket. Not for the first time I regretted ever telling Bernard and Adam about the first conversation that I had overheard. Before I joined them, I went over to the reception desk where I saw David West waiting, calm and polite as usual, not at all like a man who had been searching his guests' rooms. He smiled, and I wondered, for a brief second, whether, like me, it was a smile he practised in a mirror or something more genuine.

'Good evening, Eve. I hope you enjoyed your dinner?'

'Oh yes, thank you, excellent food. I'm not surprised you have a Michelin star. Everything about your hotel is excellent. You certainly go the extra mile for your customers.' I stared at him, hoping he would understand that I was attempting to thank him for helping me. Then, I took a small velvet box from my handbag. 'I wonder if I could leave this box in the hotel safe?'

David took the box from me quickly, and disappeared into the office behind the desk. When he returned he gave me a form to sign and I added the words, thank you, under my signature. Then, David leant toward me over the desk, 'I'm sorry to hear from Jilly that there was a broken glass at the table where you took your Champagne. I hope it didn't worry you at all?' His face was now creased with concern and I answered quickly.

'Goodness, your Jilly is a fast worker. How did you know about that already? No, no problem at all. Just a little accident when another of your guests put his glass down rather too heavily. No, problem at all, I assure you.' With a last smile and nod, I turned away from the desk and went to join Adam and Bernard. They were sitting side by side on a large leather sofa, watching me. They both stood as I drew near, and I suddenly resumed my interest in the matter of the Ferrari men. Now I couldn't wait to hear if Bernard and David had found anything of interest in the room search.

'Shall we go along to my suite and order some coffee from room service?'

'Are you seriously asking me back to your room for coffee, Princess? I thought you'd never ask. Does Bernard have to come, too?' Adam was laughing at me and seemed to have resumed his usual jokiness. Then in a quiet voice, he added, 'Did you talk with the charming concierge?'

'No, not really, I just asked him to put something in the hotel safe.'

Adam looked at me in surprise, 'But I thought... your ring?'

'Well, I had a replica made before I sold the ring my father gave me. The jeweller in Hatton Garden made it for me. It's the usual thing.'

'Of course, absolutely an everyday thing, Princess.' Adam shrugged and added, 'In your life, anyway.'

Then we had reached the first-floor corridor and were walking past rooms twenty-one and twenty-two. Bernard was walking behind us, and I turned to him and he just gave a small nod of his head. I don't know what I expected but I had felt my knees weaken at the thought that Bernard had actually been searching the rooms just a short time before. We carried on in silence until we reached my room door, and I slipped the card into the lock quickly. Bernard closed the door behind us and we all stood for a moment in silence. Then Adam threw himself into one of the armchairs and said,

'For pity's sakes, Bernie, put me out of my misery and tell me how it went.'

My suite consisted of a small lounge off the large bedroom and I took the other armchair and beckoned to the sofa, 'Adam's right, Bernard, sit down and tell us everything.'

'Is not so much to tell. David West is a good man, he is searching the rooms very carefully, but is thinking always that the men plan to steal your ring, Eve. Me, I am looking for other things and I find. *Bien sur*. Shall I order the coffee, Mademoiselle Eve?'

I let out a small gasp of exasperation, 'I shall order the coffee myself, Bernard. You had better tell us more and you can jolly well stop calling me Mademoiselle, too.'

Bernard gave a small apologetic laugh and continued, '*Très bien*, Eve. I see you are determined to know everythings, but is not much more. In the room of the Irishman, Mick, I notice a hand scanner and some papers about microchips for the horses. A list of names and some calculations printed from a computer. There is a laptop, but I had no chance to copy and download the hard disc. Is pity.'

Adam and I looked at each other, lost for words so I picked up the phone and ordered coffees. Adam shook his head, his long, blonde hair shimmering and disconcerting me even more.

'Did you say it was a pity you couldn't copy the guy's hard disc, Bernie? How did you even think of that?'

Bernard gave a classic Gallic shrug of his broad shoulders, 'Is normal, *c'est normale, n'est ce pas*?'

Adam now ran his hands back through his hair and then held his head in his hands. 'There I was thinking I had led a scandalous life, but in the last half hour I've found that the Princess thinks it's quite usual to have a diamond ring faked...' He shook his head and then held it again, 'Although I can't say I think it right that anyone as beautiful as my Princess should wear a ringer of a ring. But, I'll sort that out one day. As for you, Bernie, the perfect quiet chauffeur... you are quite prepared to sneak into a hotel room and download information. Usual and normal in my little life is having a quiet coffee after dinner'

There was a quiet tap on the door and Bernard jumped up quickly and went to open it. A young boy brought in a tray of coffee and set it on the table between us. I thanked him, tipped him too generously and he quickly left the room. I watched as Adam poured the coffee into the three cups. He was right, of course, a normal life to one person was not the same as to another. Before I could get lost in my thoughts on the matter, Bernard broke the silence.

'One thing that worried David West very much was that he found a gun in the drawer of the Mr Rupert. This is not so normal in lifes, I think.'

23

Adam and I had been stunned to silence by Bernard's words. I repeated him, my voice sounding distant in my ears.

'A gun?'

Adam added in a quiet voice, 'A loaded gun?'

'Yes, *exactement.*' Bernard answered quietly, 'Is not good thing. I think to take the bullets, but David say no, no, no. *Naturellement*, I must agree. It was up to him, only him. I think is his business and is his hotel. He was already very good to let me search the room with him. Certainly, if I take the bullets then this Mr Rupert he knows and maybe he blame the staff.'

I let out a quiet breath, 'Can't we call the police right now?'

'David say is difficult now as we have broken into room. He was very clever and had a plan ready if they came back to their rooms to say it was a check for electrical fault... but, well, I think these men are dangerous. We must think carefully. Another thing… David, he checks the balcony doors.'

I looked up sharply, 'What do you mean?'

Adam stood up, 'You're just a few rooms along from their rooms, Eve. The balconies...' Suddenly he crossed the room, opened the doors to my own balcony and disappeared through the curtains. Bernard stood up almost as quickly, but he was too late to stop Adam. Then, he turned to me.

'I think Adam is going to try the balconies.' We both rushed outside onto the small balcony and, in the dark, I could just make out the figure of Adam, already three balconies along. I clutched Bernard's arm, 'Is he mad? What does he think he's doing?'

'Now he is nearly on the Mr Rupert balcony, I think.' Bernard was straining to see in the gloom. There was some light shining from the terrace below, but there was no moonlight. The rain had stopped but heavy clouds obscured the moon. Adam turned to us and waved, then turned and took a great leap and landed like a cat on the next balcony along. He waved again and raised a thumb in triumph. I let go of Bernard's arm and turned away, unable to watch any longer. I went back inside the room and sat down feeling chilled and nauseous. The whole matter had careered completely out of control. I reached out for my coffee, but found my hand was shaking too much to be able to pick up the cup. Then, the curtains swung open and Adam jumped into the middle of the little lounge.

'The first two balconies are easy but the third and fourth, the ones before Rupert's room are a very long stretch. I don't think either of the Ferrari guys would risk the leap. Not at all likely.'

'But you did, just like that? Are you insane, Adam? You could have slipped so easily. I can't even think about it without feeling faint.'

'Well, that's because you're a Princess and it's not the sort of thing that Princesses do, or even think about. Here, have a butterscotch. The sugar will make you feel better.'

I took the sweet silently and, as the honey flavour filled my mouth, I did indeed feel a little better. Bernard came back into the room and sat down beside me.

'So, Adam, could you see in the room?'

'Just through a crack between the curtains. Rupe is fast asleep snoring in bed. In the next room, Mick is drinking from a whisky flask and reading the Sporting News. His curtains weren't pulled across. I'm damned sure neither of them could climb the balconies. Neither of them are the slightest bit fit.'

'What is all this talk?' I ran my fingers through my hair, 'Will you both just stop for a minute. I think we have to tell the police, not necessarily your friend in the Met, Bernard, but at least the local constabulary.'

'But, Eve, we have absolutely nothing to tell them. Just suspicions... even the gun... Rupert may well have a licence for it.'

'I suppose... so what on earth do we do?'

'First, you should pack a night bag and change rooms with me or Bernard.'

'I most certainly will not.' I glared at Adam, 'I'm not going to move rooms for them.'

'I think is good idea, Eve. Is a good plan.' Bernard stood up and went to close the windows.' The locks are no very secure. David agreed that.'

'Well, I'll close the shutters, too. I am not moving out.'

'Alternatively, I could sleep here with you? Sound like a perfect solution to me.' Adam gave a lop-sided grin, 'Or maybe Bernard could sleep across your royal doorstep?'

'Don't be ridiculous, Adam. I'm not afraid. Now get out, both of you. I'm dropping with exhaustion and I'm going to bed... alone, thank you.'

24

'After you chucked us out last night, Bernard and I went through everything he had seen in the Ferrari rooms.'

I looked at Adam wearily as he spoke, and saw his face was unusually serious. Perhaps he was as tired as I was after a long night of poor sleep. I had insisted on staying in my room alone, but had then spent hours trying to fall asleep. I had read an entire book on my Kindle and then drifted into a light doze, only to be awoken by a small noise outside. I had stayed in bed, frozen with fear, my heart thumping and my mind imagining the shutters bursting open and the oily Rupert standing over me, wielding a gun. Of course, nothing of the sort had happened, but then I had begun to go over the chain of events of the last few days in Suffolk. Round and round in my head until I felt giddy with fear and felt a wave of panic rising inside me. So, no, I had not slept well and now, listening to Adam as he carried on telling me about racehorse microchips, hand-held scanners and betting odds... all things that were utterly outside my field of knowledge... right now, I could happily have slid back into my chair and fallen into a deep sleep. But Bernard was talking to me,

'You look very tired, Mademoiselle Eve. Are you sure you want to go to the Fellowes' again this morning?'

I was brought out of my sleepy state with a start at his words. Of course, I had quite forgotten that I had asked him to make me another appointment. Yes, the Fellowes' sparkling wine. I sat up straight in my chair again,

'No, I'm absolutely fine. What time are we due there?'

'Sara suggested about eleven. Now is time to go or I must phone her?' Bernard was still looking at me closely and frowning. 'If you're tired I can call and cancel?'

'Didn't I just say that I was absolutely fine, Bernard?' My voice was waspish and angry and I felt immediately ashamed that my tiredness had caused me to be so rude. 'Sorry, Bernard, very sorry. You're right, I am a bit tired, but I think the chaos of the last few days is beginning to get to me. I think we should all go to the Fellowes and wrap up this chapter and get out of Newmarket as soon as we can.'

'I'm all for that, Princess, although only yesterday you decided not to use the Fellowes' story. Anyway, you don't need me to come with you this morning, do you? I've taken more photos at the Fellowes' place than you can ever need. I had thought to go and see Toni and Miss Mopp.'

Having just been unnecessarily abrupt with Bernard, I hesitated before answering Adam. I didn't want to order or beg him to come with me, as I knew it would trigger one of our ridiculous rows. But I was too tired to be tactful and much too tired to argue. Adam spoke again before I could reply,

'I can see by the Princess pout that I am under royal command. Don't worry, your majesty, I'll come with you, noblesse oblige and all that.'

I sighed and wondered why it was that he always knew what I was thinking. I had called him a magician, but maybe he was a mind-reader, too. I pushed my hair back behind my ears and tried to sound reasonable,

'The thing is, sheerly by chance, the sparkling wine that the Ferrari men gave me to taste last night... well, to my astonishment it turned out to come from the Fellowes' vineyards. I can't think why on earth they hadn't offered it to me to taste. It's a very fine wine, one of the best English sparkling wines I've ever tasted. I was interested the moment I saw the tiny, persistent bubbles spiralling up the flute. It's fruity and yet racy, with such an elegant finish that...'

'Stop right there, Princess, I beg you. Let's just go. I can tell you're getting your usual energy back. Please, no wine talk, just take me and my camera anywhere you wish but don't talk about fizz. The only part that sounded good was the elegant finish. That I can really hang on to. Ah, an elegant finish...' He looked at me, his eyes turning to the strangely intense, darker blue that they did at times. 'In fact, any finish would do, elegant or otherwise.'

Bernard stood up, '*On y va?* Perhaps we are not long at the Fellowes' and then I can take you to meet your girlfriend, Adam?'

I looked up sharply and then realised that Bernard was talking of Miss Mopp. Adam smiled happily,

'Fine idea, Bernie, I can handle two stroppy mares in one morning if I try. Which reminds me, I haven't asked you about Elaine for a while. How is your long-distance romance going on?'

The two men walked ahead of me, chatting and jibing at each other. I followed slowly, thinking about how I would write up the sparkling wine story and include Sara's cookery classes. Yes, there had to be some mileage to be had out of the place, and I knew the photos were excellent. They always were. Adam had not been bragging when he had said he had some landscapes photos that had a Gainsborough or Constable quality. I sighed, not just tired, but exasperated that the long-haired blonde young man sauntering along in front of me could be so talented and so very annoying.

25

'Didn't you see Hugo at the Royal Park this morning?'

Sara was standing at her school kitchen work bench, up to her elbows in flour. When we had arrived at the manor, there had not been anyone to greet us, not even the black Labrador. We had wandered around to the barn complex and eventually found Sara at work alone, with the dog asleep in front of the Aga. 'He had a meeting there this morning with a potential client. I told him you would be here at eleven. He should be back by now.' Sara raised her elbow to her forehead and stopped work for a minute. It was as though she was attempting to brush away the lines that furrowed her forehead. I felt a rush of sympathy for her as it seemed that she was almost overwhelmed.

'Oh, please don't worry, Sara. We only made the appointment on the spur of the moment. I expect we just missed Hugo en route.'

Sara looked at me in relief and gave a smile that I thought was probably as practised as my own. She went to the sink and rinsed her hands, 'Can I offer you a coffee... maybe a slice of my latest almond cake?'

'Thanks, but I was wondering... if you could just point us in the right direction... if we could walk and find the vines that produce your sparkling wine. I tasted it by chance, last night at the Royal Park.'

Sara turned around and looked surprised and anxious at the same time, 'Oh, I don't think Hugo would want you to write about it. He says it's not of good quality, and he is going to change it completely. It's his next project in his lab. I think he's analysing it after this year's harvest.'

'But it's perfect. Probably the best sparkling English wine I've ever tasted.' I spoke before I considered that my announcement would undermine Hugo's expertise. Now, Sara put her hand up to her mouth in complete amazement.

'Is that true? I mean, you're the expert but... well, it's the only wine we produce that is from the original stock that my Grandmother planted. Hugo hasn't had time to change it yet... oh dear...' She faltered to a halt.

There was an embarrassing silence in the kitchen, and the dog stirred as though aware that something was slightly wrong. Adam went over to the Aga and stroked the dog and said,

'Well, I was tempted by the cake and coffee, Sara, but maybe we could take this lazy lab out for a run and just take a look at these vines. As far as grapes go, in my experience, Eve Sinclair certainly knows her onions.'

Sara laughed and looked relieved at the lightening of the atmosphere. 'I'm sure she does. Gosh, I could do with a break and some fresh air, let's take a walk.' She pulled off her apron and went to the door and took a well-worn oiled jacket from a hook. She seemed suddenly filled with a new energy... or maybe it was new hope. We followed her out into the yard. The light mist was lifting, and there was a little watery sunshine.

'This Suffolk weather is a new challenge every day,' Adam pulled out his camera, 'We were scheduled to be in Pompeii this week, where I'm sure the sky is a solid regulation daily blue, but here... this is very beautiful.'

'Pompeii, goodness, I'm afraid the manor can't compete with that...' Suddenly she laughed aloud, and her face showed all the prettiness of youth, 'In fact, as far as ruins go, we can probably match it. No volcano, just the disastrous Hugo effect.'

We all drew to halt in the middle of the yard and suddenly Sara went over to a bench and sat down, her head in her hands. Adam and Bernard looked at me in concern, and I nodded. I knew that I would be able to talk to Sara more easily on my own. I spoke quietly to Adam,

'I'm fairly sure you'll find the oldest vines on the top south slopes. It's the area we haven't yet walked through. Do you mind?'

Adam nodded quickly, 'Not at all, Bernie and I will go ahead. Do I mind? Gosh, Princess, that was almost not a royal command.' He smiled cheekily and patted me on the top of my head and walked away before I could reply. Bernard gave me a small nod, too and followed Adam. I watched them go for a moment, the Labrador had decided to stay close to Adam... and who could blame it?

I turned and went to sit down beside Sara who was now calmly staring into space. We sat side by side on the stone bench in silence for a moment, but it felt companionable. Then Sara began to speak, her voice calm and quiet,

'I'm sure you know by now, Eve, we're teetering on the brink of bankruptcy... again. It's the talk of the county, I know.'

I remained silent, and Sara continued, 'Hugo is a disaster, I know that, but he's my disaster. I don't know if you can understand that? You're very young.'

'Hmm, well, I may be young, but I know something about financial disaster.'

'Oh, I'm so sorry, how tactless of me, of course, you do. Your famous father.'

'Infamous, more like. But never mind that, I'm over it now. You are in the middle of your problems, it seems to me.'

'Oh dear, you don't know the half of it. If you only knew how good it is to let go and actually talk about it.'

'Talk on, Sara. I'm here to listen, and I think I can help.'

Sara looked at me then, straight in the eye and I think I saw another glimmer of new courage.

26

'For a royal princess, I think you're doing a grand job as a shrink.'

We were back in the Mercedes and on our return journey to the Royal Park. Adam was sitting beside me in the back, and I had already recounted my conversation with Sara Fellowes. Adam looked at me, his dark blonde eyebrows raised as he continued,

'Do you really think you can help promote their sparkling wine then?'

'Definitely, I have every confidence in it and all they need to do is to produce more and to be fastidiously careful with management of the canopy to avoid rot. I've told Sara they will have to harvest early to get clean fruit. She's ready to get to grips with it all, and insist that more of their Chardonnay and Pinot Noir grapes are used in the traditional Champagne method... they already do it all perfectly in the old way... *tirage, remouage, dégorgement, dosage*. They've been doing it the same way since her Sara's grandmother started at the manor. It's such a good story now. Did you manage to get any good photos of the *pupitres*?'

Adam leant forward and spoke to Bernard, 'Would you translate, Bernie, the Princess has gone all Frenchified in her excitement.'

I gave an exasperated sigh and dug Adam in the ribs, 'You know exactly what I'm talking about, Adam. You were as excited as I was when we went down to the cellars beneath the manor house. That long line of *pupitres*, very well, the old oak wine racks... tell me you have some good photos.'

'You can be so unkind, Princess. How can you doubt that I would let you down when you're like a little Pocahontas on the hot scent of a story. Of course, I have the most amazing candlelit shots of the old oak racks, if that's what you mean. Here, take a look-see.'

Adam handed me his camera, and I scrolled through the last twenty or so frames. I had to admit that I had been unjust if not unkind. There were at least ten excellent moody photos to choose from. I passed the camera back,

'Phew, I'm just so relieved. I think I can see the light at the end of the tunnel as far as this sixth and final chapter goes. I know Hugo won't like it, but I think Sara is finally ready to face up to him. With my sponsorship, they can sell as much sparkling wine as they can produce at a high price. I've agreed to sign the label once the quality control is in place. But Sara has to insist that Hugo doesn't mess around with it in his wretched laboratory.'

'Princess, I'm proud of you. I think you may have saved the Fellowes' skin and miraculously brewed up a good story, too.'

I felt ridiculously pleased with Adam's praise and enjoyed a happy glow of my own self-satisfaction. Then I remembered. The gun-carrying Ferrari men. We were nearly back at the Royal Park, and my tiredness suddenly returned.

'Thank you, Adam. The photos are perfect and wil be just the right contrast to the misty landscapes. I think the chapter will be one of our best. Did you want to go on with Bernard to the stables to meet up with Toni? I think I'll go back to the spa and relax.'

Adam looked at me doubtfully, 'Do you think you're safe?'

'Safe? What can happen to me in the spa?'

Bernard interrupted. 'I think is the good idea if I leave Adam at the stables and then take you to the spa. Is best way, no?'

I didn't answer for a minute as I considered the matter. In one way I thought it was ridiculous to be worried about my safety, but in another way, I knew I would feel happier to have Bernard parked outside, somewhere near at hand. Before I could make a decision, it was made for me as Bernard swung the car into a lay-by

'I leave you here, Adam, you like to walk, and even you have your shoes on and dry. *Mais oui*, if you cross the next two paddocks, you are already at Toni's stables. I see it on the map.'

'Good idea, Bernie. That's fine.'

Before I could say a word, Adam had jumped out of the car and Bernard pulled away again. I turned to look out of the rear window and saw Adam leaping over a five-bar gate and heading across a grassy paddock. I rested my hand on the leather seat and felt the residual heat from where he had been sitting just seconds before. It wasn't the first time that he had left the Mercedes abruptly and chosen to walk, but there was no doubt about it, I missed him.

27

I forced myself to swim a fast twenty lengths before heading to the massage room. I wanted to thoroughly tire myself physically, to match my mental exhaustion. After the success of the morning at the Fellowes, I felt suddenly depressed. I was too drained to even begin to think about the Ferrari men and what on earth they could be planning. The spa receptionist had booked me in for a massage with Lois, and I had half an hour to swim. As I moved swiftly through the warm turquoise water of the pool, I tried to untangle the knot of confused ideas in my head. Why was my invitation to the Saturday race meeting so annoying to the Ferrari men? The only possible answer that I could come up with was the one we had already discussed over and over again. My appearance at the race course would excite a lot of media interest. I had been asked to present one of the cups, cameras would be flashing, and reporters would be doing what they do best, pushing and shoving their microphones at me. I swam underwater for a few strokes and tried once again to stop my brain worrying and fretting about it all. Maybe, I should just call off sick and turn down the invitation. My agent would be disappointed, angry even, but so what? We could be back in London by tomorrow lunch time, and I could call a meeting with her to discuss the changes in the last chapter. Then, I opened my eyes under water and looked into the shimmering blue... then I could fly back to Provence to work through the whole manuscript.

I surfaced and saw that Lois was waiting for me at the corner of the pool. I raised a hand in greeting and pulled myself out of the water. I was pleased to see her. At least it stopped me thinking onward to the idea that Adam might accompany me to Provence. Would he have other work to get on with when he was back in London, would he resume his life as a war photographer? I flicked back my wet hair and blinked... yes, I was glad to see Lois.

'Hi, Lois, sorry if I'm late.'

Lois held out a towelling robe to me and gave a small smile of welcome but said nothing. We went together into one of the massage rooms, and I stretched out on the bed. Lois covered me with a warm towel, and I felt the comfort of the heated bed under me. I closed my eyes, glad that Lois was unusually silent. The soothing aroma of jasmine and sandalwood filled the air, and I relaxed. Lois worked slowly along the line of my spine, smoothing away the knots of tension. I lay down, my face fitting comfortably into the gap in the massage bench, and almost drifted off to sleep, listening to the quiet strains of Tibetan bells. I had never seriously learnt how to meditate, but I had taken yoga lessons for some years, and now I began to feel a wonderful floaty feeling. I was just about to truly give way to total relaxation when I heard the stifled sound of a sob. My brain flashed back into action, and I wondered, hoped too, that I had imagined it. I laid still, Lois was working across my shoulders, her hands moving rhythmically without any hesitation. But no, there it was again, a quiet sob, almost a hiccough. Now I could feel a slight tremor in her hands. I let out a long breath of something mixed between exasperation and disbelief. What was it that Adam and Bernard had teased me about? Hearing a woman crying? They were right, it had led me into trouble in Frascati and before that in Savoie. Could it really be that Lois, usually so bubbly and talkative, was now crying? I thought about ignoring the sound and closed my eyes tight, but it was no good. It was impossible to shut my ears to the soft sobbing sound. I opened my eyes and stared down at the white tiled floor and then spoke into the space in the massage bed.

'Are you all right, Lois?' There I had said it and, of course, she wasn't. The squeakiness of her voice as she replied made that very evident.

'I'm sorry, Eve. I just can't help crying, I'm in such a fix.'

Reluctantly I turned over and sat up, wrapping the warm towel around me. I swung my feet down to the floor and looked at Lois. As I suspected her eyes were red-rimmed, tears were streaming down her cheeks and the tip of her small nose was bright pink.

'Do you want to tell me about it, Lois?' I said the words, but my heart wasn't in it. Hadn't I just had a heartfelt talk with Sara Fellowes? This woman to woman stuff just wasn't my forte. Even though I had felt smugly pleased that Adam had praised me for helping Sara, now, all I wanted was to sleep, all on my own, in a luxuriously warm bed for hours and hours. I tried hard not to sigh aloud and stifled a yawn as Lois began to speak.

'It's T-t -t Toni.' Lois managed to stutter out the name, and I tried not to look as though I wasn't at all surprised. The young farrier was an outstandingly handsome young man and.... before I could follow my train of thought, Lois managed to continue between sobs,'

'He's...sob... put all ... sob, sob... our savings... sob... on that sob horse.'

Now, that I hadn't expected although, of course, I should have. Toni had already talked about the idea at our pub lunch. I just hadn't really believed that anyone would actually do it. Surely it was madly reckless?

'Oh dear.' I managed a reply but it was hardly adequate and not at all comforting, so it was not very surprising that Lois broke down into a gale of weeping. She crumpled up on the floor, and I looked down at her in dismay, wondering what on earth I could do? I decided to be firm and haughty, at least it came naturally to me.

'Now, come along. Lois. Pull yourself together. You're supposed to be at work, and I'm getting a bit cold.'

To my relief, my admonishing words did the trick Lois jumped up immediately and fetched me a fresh warm towelling robe and wrapped it around me. I decided to grab the moment and continue in the same vein. 'Now, I'd love a manicure, and I see you have a little counter over there. Help me choose a shade, and we can have a chat while you do my nails.'

Further relief on my behalf as Lois obediently went over to the make-up bar and pulled out a range of nail colours. We discussed the merits of Passionate Peach against Ballerina Pink for several minutes, and then she began the manicure.

'I'm ever so sorry, Eve, I've never been unprofessional before and in front of you, of all people, my first real celeb. Will you have to say anything to the management?'

'Good gracious, no, of course not. I quite understand what it's like to be under pressure and financial risk.' I hesitated as I thought about the truth in my own words for a moment. 'You must be in shock, too. I mean, did you agree to Toni placing such a bet?'

'No, no, I didn't.' Lois looked completely baffled and as tired as I felt myself, 'He tried to persuade me that it was a dead cert, but then we agreed not to risk our money. That's what I thought, anyway.'

'I don't know anything about bookies or racing but is there any way you can get the money back?'

Lois looked at me with a pitying smile, 'You must be joking, Eve. No, the money's all on Miss Mopp and that's that.'

'I see, well then there is nothing to do but cross your fingers, I suppose. I am sorry, Lois.'

Lois stopped filing my nails for a moment and tears welled up in her eyes again. 'That's not all, Eve. There's something even worse. I've been ever so stupid.'

I looked at her anxiously, wondering what there could possibly be worse or more stupid than her hard-earned savings riding on the back of an unruly racehorse.

'What do you mean, Lois?'

She took a long shuddering breath and said, almost in a whisper, 'Hugo Fellowes was here this morning for a massage, and I told him what Toni had done. He was very kind and listened for a bit and then he asked if Toni had it from a hot tip at the stables. I told him that I supposed so and he looked sort of pleased. It wasn't until after he'd gone that I remembered there's a story around that he has a gambling problem.'

28

'She didn't?' Adam looked at me aghast, 'But it wa
Lois that told us that Hugo was known to be a compulsive
gambler. How could she be so stupid?'

We were sitting on the terrace of the Royal Park,
drinking tea, and I had told Adam about my talk with Lois
The sun was now hot, and the flagstones were steaming
after all the heavy rain. I was feeling good after a couple o
hours undisturbed sleep in my new suite. While I had beer
in the spa, Bernard had taken it upon himself to have the
hotel staff change my room. At first, I had been rather
annoyed but, seeing the look of solid determination in
Bernard's eyes, I had given in. In fact, the new suite was
very comfortable, probably a honeymoon suite, and
certainly, I had felt more secure than being a few balconie
away from a gun in a drawer. Now, I flicked back my
newly shampooed hair and enjoyed the warmth of the sun
on my face. I was fortunate to have skin that tanned easily
and, although I was careful to wear plenty of expensive
sun cream, I never had to worry about turning pink. I
thought about answering Adam but felt no inclination to d
so, and then he continued,

'Don't just flick your hair back and do the Garbo
thing, Eve. What are we going to do?'

My relaxed good mood was sliding away from m
rising into the air like the mist from the wet flagstones.

'Do? What can we do, Adam? Why do we have to
do anything?' I picked up my teacup and began to sip the
very pleasant and delicate Lapsang Souchong. It had a fin
smoky-pine flavour, and I breathed in the perfume. Yes,
most certainly Formosan, a tea that my father had
introduced me to when I was quite young. He had always
drunk Lapsang. I smiled as I remembered him telling me
that it was a favourite of Winston Churchill and that if it
was good enough for him then... my thoughts drifted on
pleasantly, imagining my father now, on the Malabar coas
in the Arabian Ocean, possibly drinking the local brew. M
last postcard from him, forwarded to me from my

housekeeper in Provence, had been slightly different from the usual few words I received every month. I carried the card now in my handbag, and I was tempted to take it out and show it to Adam. The few extra words, after his usual greeting, had been enigmatic, cryptic maybe, but had made no sense to me. My father, a devotee of the Times crossword, could have been giving me a clue to decipher. Maybe Adam would be able to make something of the words. I smiled and opened my bag but then Adam spoke,

'Now you look more like the Cheshire Cat than Garbo. Smiling your bloomin' mysterious smile. Eve, will you answer me or not?' Adam's heated words broke into my pleasant perfumed reminiscence, and I frowned at him,

'You never give up, do you, Adam? Can't I just sit in this gentle English sunshine and enjoy my tea?'

I snapped my handbag shut again, 'Why do we have to worry about other people's problems? I don't see there is anything we can do, anyway.'

Adam stood up quietly and walked away from the terrace.

I looked after him as he went, resisting the desire to throw my teacup at his broad-shouldered arrogant back. I poured myself another cup of tea and took a small sip. Now the delicate flavour had turned bitter, the leaves stewing too long in the pot. I sat, smouldering with suppressed anger in the warm sun. If Adam Wright thought I would go after him, then he was very mistaken. Always so righteous, yes, perfect name for him, Mr Always Wright. I sat very still, aware that there were several eyes staring at me as usual. The last thing I needed was for any hint of a row between myself and Adam to be flashed across the celebrity gossip. My agent was already delighted with the rumour being spread that Adam Wright, young eminent photographer, was close-up and friendly with me. Well, I certainly didn't feel friendly toward him right now, nor were we close-up. I was fuming with rage at the way he always thought he knew best. The way he made me feel I wasn't doing the right thing. Mr Wright, always so right. I suppressed a sob that could have brought tears to eyes. I relaxed my shoulders and decided I would sit calmly for a few more minutes and then... but then my mobile rang.

'Mademoiselle Eve, I have news from my friend, Colin at the Met. I am parked near the terrace. Do you see me?'

I took in a deep breath, relieved to hear Bernard's calm voice and to know that he was nearby. I glanced over to the car park and saw the shiny Mercedes parked in a corner. Bernard had been watching over me as usual. I raised a hand and waved. Never mind that Colin's news might not be of any interest to me, I was pleased to be back with Bernard. I was sure that he would understand that I didn't want to know any more about the Ferrari men and mad gamblers. I just wanted to go back to London and then to Provence. I walked quickly over to the car, blotting out the thought that I had hoped to go to Provence with Adam. Bernard jumped out of the car as I approached and opened the rear door.

'I think I'll sit up-front with you, Bernard. We can talk better.'

'*Bien sur, Mademoiselle Eve.*' Bernard quickly opened the front passenger door, and I slipped into the comfort of the soft grey leather. I didn't remind Bernard that he was now supposed to call me Eve. His familiar French-accented voice sounded good, and his usual *bien sur* had the comfort of a warm blanket. I rested my head back on the headrest and felt my anger subside. Adam Wright was right about one thing, Bernard was a saint and always came to my rescue. I allowed my brain to concede a point to Adam, and then began to think about our latest row. No, he couldn't possibly be right in that case. As though Bernard had guessed what I was thinking, he said,

'I see Adam leave the terrace. He had his determined face on. How do you say? *Un homme chargé d'une mission.*'

'A man on a mission? Oh dear, I think you're right Bernard. He's in his brave knight mode.'

'Brave night?

'No, no, knight, *chevalier*... you know, *il va aider une demoiselle en détresse*. Lois is in trouble, and Adam is off like Sir Galahad to rescue a damsel in distress.'

'I know nothing of this story. Where is Adam now? I seeing him walking fast up the drive of the hotel. Where is he going?'

'I have no idea. He just went off.' I answered, the residual anger in my voice turning to misery.

'Ah, so you make war again with Adam. Tut tut, always you are going mad at each other. *Dis donc*, now is not the time to argue. I have news from Colin, he has been working for us at the Met.'

'Not more about the wretched Ferrari men, Bernard. I think we should just leave it all alone. Even poor Lois and Toni's risky bet... I don't want to be here to see Miss Mopp race. And now Lois has passed on the hot tip to Hugo Fellowes so, doubtless, he will place the equivalent of a small Gainsborough on the horse. I think life in Newmarket is just too crazy for me. I'll be happy to write up a glowing review of the Fellowes' lovely sparkling wine and Sara's excellent cookery school... but that's me finished. Enough, *suffis*.'

My words fell into a silence and Bernard seemed to be thinking. When he made no reply after another quiet minute, I began protesting again.

'I mean, Bernard, you must agree, these problems are not my problems. I want to leave Newmarket first thing tomorrow and...'

My speech was interrupted by my mobile ringing again. I snatched it up, hoping it would be Adam calling, maybe apologising? We usually made up quickly after one of our rows. I sighed when I saw it was my agent, Melanie, ringing. I was tempted to ignore the call but, in fact, I was relieved to be interrupted. My speech to Bernard had a ring of protesting too much. I took the call.

'Hi, Melanie, how are you?'

29

My short phone call with Melanie quickly ruined my chance of leaving Newmarket before the Saturday races. She had been excitedly overcome by her own success at arranging a TV interview on the big day. I was to be wined and dined by the Jockey Club dignitaries, and then interviewed and probably thoroughly annoyed by a string of personal questions that I would dodge answering She worked so hard on my behalf that I was quite unable to turn the whole dreadful thing down. I owed her too much, and I was very aware that my success depended just as much on her as my own ability. Yes, I could recognise a wine, but I was about as useless as a chocolate teapot when it came to networking. Flesh-pressing, as Melanie horribly described it, made my own skin creep.

Now, I flicked through the clothes hanging in my wardrobe at the Royal Park. Friday afternoon and probably too late to go shopping. I would have to find something suitable from my wardrobe. I flicked the hangers back in the reverse direction, but nothing shouted Newmarket race meeting and TV interview.

I sat on the bed and decided that I felt thoroughly miserable. I had heard nothing from Adam. Bernard had spent half an hour trying to interest me in the information he had from his friend Colin. It appeared that the oily Rupert Breville had nothing too murky in his past. He had a small stud and training establishment in Ireland, but was not often seen at the races. Mick, on the other hand, was a well-known punter at race courses across Britain, although his business was in London, where he was the managing director of an IT company. He apparently had a record with the police, something to do with illegally transferring money abroad. I had tried to listen to Bernard, but I found the whole subject boring. I had never been interested in my own father's affairs, and I was even less likely to care about this Mick Flanagan. If he had committed a crime in the past then presumably he had paid his dues. My lack of concentration was partly due to most of my brain waiting for a call from Adam. Bernard finally gave up on me, and we agreed to go to our rooms for an hour or so and meet later in the bar. Both of us, I think, silently hoping that Adam would be back by then.

Now, I stretched out on the bed and looked at the ceiling. I thought about starting work on my notes on the Fellowes' chapter, but I had no real energy for it. Then, the phone beside my bed rang. I snatched it up, momentarily wondering why Adam would call the room rather than my mobile. But, of course, it wasn't Adam.

'Hi, Lois, are you all right?'

'I'm OK, well better anyway. I just wanted to phone and apologise to you, Eve. I'm so sorry I broke down like that. I shouldn't have... so unprofessional.'

'Don't worry about it for a second, Lois. I quite understand. You must be so anxious and yet there is nothing you can do but wait it out. I'm so sorry.'

'You're so kind, Eve. Thank you for being so understanding. I had a row with Toni, and now he's disappeared. He's not at the stables or...'

I heard her voice begin to break and I guessed she was holding back another storm of tears. I spoke quickly,

'Adam's not around either, perhaps they're together... boys will be boys.' I could hardly believe that I had said that. What did I know about boys being anything? But at least it seemed to have cheered Lois a little, and dammed the flood of pending tears for a moment. I continued in the same vein, 'Do you know what, Lois? I think girls should be girls sometimes, too.'

'What do you mean, Eve?' Lois' voice was much perkier now, and she sounded interested.

'I've just had a great idea. I know there's not much time, but how about we go shopping together. A little retail therapy? I need something to wear tomorrow. Is there a good clothes shop in Newmarket?'

'Well, there are a few... ' Lois now sounded decidedly chirpy, 'Do you really mean you want me to go shopping with you?'

'Yes, if you can get away from work?'

'Oh, I'm not on shift until Monday now. Really, Eve, you mean me... go shopping with you?'

'Absolutely but we'd have to hurry, and I'll have to get Bernard to drive us. What time do the shops close?'

'I can pick you up in my Mini if that would be all right. I've just thought, it's late closing in Cambridge, we could go there if you wanted.'

'Brilliant, let's do that. I'll be down in reception in ten minutes.'

I put down the phone and felt a surge of energy and sheer pleasure at the idea of a shopping spree. I checked my mobile and saw there was still no message or missed call from Adam. Well, if he were sulking then he would have to sulk a bit longer. I called Bernard and wasted five minutes persuading him that I would be perfectly all right in the company of Lois and being driven in her Mini. Then, I ran a brush hastily through my hair and pulled on a hat. I looked in the mirror and smiled at myself. How ridiculous that I had to behave like a movie star. Just a few TV programmes and my life had become public interest. My long hair was certainly my most distinguishing feature, so I twisted it into a tight bun and pushed it under my baseball cap. I nodded at my image and waved myself a cheery farewell.

Lois was already waiting in the lobby, and we dashed out together, almost running to her car. I think we both felt as though we were escaping. I don't remember feeling like it since I had once play hooky from school to go to a polo match. Now, maybe nearly ten years later, I felt the same thrill of getting away from everything that I should be doing.

Lois drove well, and we were parking in the multi storey car park by John Lewis in less than half an hour. W wandered through the mall, aimlessly at first, window-shopping and chatting. Lois had cheered up and was almost as giggly as she had been when I first met her in th pub. I found myself laughing with her and thoroughly enjoying myself. We stopped outside Fossil and Lois admired a tan leather clutch bag.

'Why don't we go in and have a look at it?' I began to walk toward the door but Lois held back.

'Oh, I couldn't, it's ever such an expensive shop. They'd all stare at me.'

'Whatever do you mean?' I looked at Lois, completely mystified. 'It's only a shop, and if the assistants look at you, it's only because they're hoping you'll buy something.'

'Yeah, but it's the sort of shop where they know I won't.'

Still puzzled, but beginning to get the drift of her way of thinking, I took her arm and almost pulled her into the shop. She was right, the staff were standing around doing very little and they did stare. Well, I was used to that.

'We'd like to see the tan clutch bag you have in the window. Is that the only colour?'

A tall girl glided toward us and, looking as though it was the last thing she wanted to do, she opened a drawer and pulled out a similar bag.

Ten minutes later I had bought the tan bag, and we made our way back out into the marble hall of the Grand Arcade. Lois was looking quite shocked.

'You were so snooty, Eve. I never thought you'd be like that.'

I took her arm, and we walked along in companionable silence as I thought about her words. An interesting first for me to be considered as unusually haughty. I wondered whether it was only Adam that found me autocratic. I checked my mobile, but there was still no message from him. Then I saw that Lois was looking at her phone too, and by the look on her face, there was nothing from Toni, either. I pushed my phone back into the bottom of my bag,

'Buck up, Lois, the shops close in an hour, and I need to find something to wear tomorrow. Let's try Robert Sayle... they must have something suitable for Ladies Day at the July Races. Something suitably horsified and yet frivolous.'

'Might be more difficult now, you'll have to find something to go with that tan bag.'

'Oh no, the bag's for you.' I tossed the carrier bag to her and enjoyed the look of delight on Lois' face.

Certainly, a little shopping could be most therapeutic at times.

30

The therapeutic glow didn't last long. Lois drove me back to the Royal Park and turned down my offer of a drink in the bar. I was quite glad as I was anxious to find Bernard and know if he had heard from Adam. I knew that Lois was feeling the same way and hoping to find Toni back in their flat at the stable, although her phone had been as blank and lifeless as mine. I waved to Lois as she drove off and then was surprised to see Bernard pulling into the car park. I ran over to greet him, awkwardly clutching the four carrier bags full of my purchases. He got out of the Mercedes quickly and opened up his umbrella. I had hardly noticed that the rain was beginning to fall again quite heavily.

'I'm just back from Cambridge...' I held out my carrier bags in proof and Bernard quickly took them from me and nodded. I looked at him, suddenly suspicious. 'Did you follow Lois and me? Did you, Bernard?'

'*Mais oui, bien sur.*' He nodded again and gave an apologetic half smile.

'Bernard Guillaume you are one cunning man. I didn't even notice the Mercedes and it's so huge. I didn't see you once.'

'Is how it has to be, Mademoiselle Eve, I not want to spoil your evening out shopping.'

'What am I to do with you, Bernard. I'd like to say you shouldn't have bothered but, I have to admit, I am truly grateful. Perhaps this is a good moment to say that, what I am trying to tell you, is that I am truly grateful for all the thousands of times you have been there in the background looking after me.'

Bernard held the umbrella over me and we made our way to the entrance to the Royal Park, both embarrassed by my little speech.

David West greeted us in the lobby, smiling and even more elegant than ever in a well-tailored tuxedo.

'Good evening, Miss Sinclair. Let me have those bags taken up to your room.' He took the bags from

Bernard and before he could even look around, a young uniformed page boy had emerged from behind a palm tree and taken the bags from David.

'Thanks, David. The Royal Park certainly knows how to spoil their guests.'

David gave a little bow of his head and looked very pleased with himself. Then he turned to Bernard,

'Have you tracked down young Adam yet?'

I looked anxiously at Bernard. So he hadn't heard from Adam either and had even asked the concierge. Bernard shook his head and frowned as David carried on talking in his calm friendly voice,

'I expect he's out on the town with Toni. As I told you earlier, Bernard, they came into the Park together and sat in one of the lounges for a while talking. Then they went off again in Toni's truck. I expect Toni is showing him around the high life or low life of Newmarket. There are plenty of bars and clubs where the stable lads and lasses spend time off.'

I spoke up quickly, 'I don't think Adam would do that. He doesn't even drink.'

David looked at me then, and spoke more seriously. 'I can see you're both worried. Leave it with me for an hour or so, and I'll send one of my staff to scout around town and report back. Is that a good idea?'

'Oh yes, if you would, please. This is so unlike Adam.' Bernard nodded in agreement, and we both thanked David and left him to it. We made our way slowly across the lobby, and I was about to collect my key card when I changed my mind.

'What do you say to a drink in the bar, Bernard. I need a long, cold fruit juice after my shopping extravaganza. I'm not used to this girly shopping stuff. I'm exhausted and dehydrated from time spent in the mall's air conditioning.'

We sat in two wing chairs in a quiet bar, and Jilly, the same barmaid who had served us before, came over to take our order. There was no waiting around at the well-run Royal Park.

'I haven't even decided what to order yet,' I smiled up at Jilly, 'I've been on the most exhausting shopping spree and need something cold, long and non-alcoholic... what do you suggest?'

'Would you like to try my own favourite... iced elderberry juice with soda water and a slice of lemon and chopped cucumber?'

'That sounds perfect. Bernard, how about you?'

'For me, an espresso. Thank you.'

Tonight, Jilly's long brown hair was twisted into a high knot that bobbed from side to side as she hurried off. I thought again how excellently every member of staff at the Royal Park looked and worked. I would be able to give a glowing recommendation in my list of places to stay at the end of chapter six. End of the final chapter and end of the book... my heart beat faster as I inevitably thought about Adam and our long-held agreement not to mix business with pleasure. But when the business was finished would there be time for pleasure? And where on earth was the man?

'Do you think Adam would be in a bar with Toni, Bernard?'

'*Non*, is not his style, I think. I am more thinking he is trying to find out more about the men with the Ferrari. He is so... how do you say, *il est le genre d'homme capable de faire une chose aussi impulsive.*'

'Yes,' I sighed heavily, 'You're right, he can be very rash.'

Jilly arrived with a silver tray with our drinks and a small bowl of olives. I sipped the cold drink and looked gratefully at Jilly. 'That's so good. Just what I needed, thank you.' Jilly blushed and nodded then seemed to hesitate.

'I heard from David that you're looking for Adam Wright. He was in this bar earlier with Toni and...' She faltered to a halt and stood, clutching her silver tray nervously in front of her.

'Did you hear them say where they might be going on to?' I asked, aware that she wouldn't want to admit to eavesdropping.

'Well, not really, but they were talking about Miss Mopp and a race tomorrow. Sorry, but I didn't really hear anything more.'

'Of course not, I quite understand, thanks anyway.'

Jilly moved away, and then turned back and added, 'Something about sleeping in the stable, too.' Then she rushed off to take an order from another guest.

I looked at Bernard in alarm, 'Sleeping in a stable Whatever are they up to?' Before Bernard could answer, the swing doors to the bar opened wide, and Adam entered the bar, his Parka hanging wetly around his shoulders. He strode up to the bar and gave Jilly and order, and then joined us at our table, dumping his wet Parka in a heap by his feet.

'Are you still angry, Princess? *Bonsoir* to you, Bernie.

I found I couldn't answer straight away. I wanted to be angry and to remind him that he was the one who ha walked off in a huff and gone missing for several hours... but I just couldn't. I was so pleased and relieved to see hir that I just sighed and shook my head. Adam turned to Bernard,

'Uh uh, Bernie, you must have heard that royal sigh. My, it's good to be back. I've had quite a time with Toni.'

Bernard, probably sensing that my anger could easily return spoke quickly, 'Where have you been, Adam what have you been doing?'

Jilly arrived with another silver tray loaded with teapot, jug and a cup and saucer. Tea at eight pm... why had I even imagined that Adam would go off on a drinkin binge?

'Ah, tea, you are a life-saver, Jilly.' I watched Adam look up at Jilly and give her a beautiful slightly lop sided smile. His loose curling hair was wet from the rain and managing to sparkle in the low light of the bar. I recognised the look and saw the effect it had on Jilly. Did he have a smile that was as professional as my own? I gave another sigh and decided this was not the time to worry about it.

'Go on then, Adam, where have you been and what have you been up to?

Adam slowly poured himself a cup of tea and sipped it before answering.

'Well, let me just say that yet again, you, Princess, overheard a woman weeping and the plot is definitely thickening.'

31

Adam gulped down four cups of tea as he hurriedly told us of his exploits and why he had been away so long. Bernard and I listened as quietly as we could, but when he said that he had searched the Ferrari men's' rooms again, I had been unable to remain silent.

'You broke into the rooms again? But how did you get the key cards? Don't tell me that David West agreed?'

'No, we decided it was too much to ask of David, so I just shinned up the wisteria from the terrace.'

I closed my eyes, trying not to visualise the height of the balcony hanging over the flagstones below or the thin wispy climbing branches on the trellis. Adam was still talking in between gulps of tea.

'That was no problem. Toni was keeping cavey in the car park in case the guys came back... he had his phone ready to buzz me.'

Bernard was looking at Adam in alarm, 'Was dangerous to do, Adam, these are men who have guns. What is this cavey?'

I interrupted, translating like an automaton, as I tried to recover my equilibrium.

'It's old British public school slang meaning 'look out'. It's the Latin word cave and so...'

'Not now, Princess.' Adam frowned at me, 'When you're not behaving like a Princess you do a fine job as a school teacher. I'm meeting Toni in twenty minutes, so if you interrupt again...'

I held my hands up in submission, and he continued as he poured the last of the dark brown tea from the pot.

'OK, so Toni was on lookout and...'

Now it was Bernard's turn to break into Adam's explanation.

'Is very dangerous to climb over that balcony and then... then how did you open the door to the bedroom?'

'Easy peasy, Bernie. You said yourself the balcony door lock was flimsy. I jemmied my credit card in, and it popped open sweet as a nut. Not even a scratch to show for it. I was pleased with that. I didn't want them to know I'd been in their rooms although...'

Now he hesitated as though deciding not to tell us something and I quickly spoke into the pause,

'But did you find anything? Any reason we can call the police? What are they up to?'

Adam drained the last of the tea from his cup and looked at me and then Bernard.

'I went through the history on the Irish Mick's laptop.'

'Didn't he have a password?'

'I was lucky with that... for some reason, I just had a hunch, and I typed in Lucky Mick, and it opened first hit.'

Bernard raised his dark eyebrows in amazement, 'Just like that? *Mon Dieu, quelle chance*!'

'Not altogether. I spent last night going over and over that conversation you recorded, Bernie. The Irish guy called himself Lucky Mick three times. Did you notice, like, 'they call me Lucky Mick'... and then, 'that's me name, Lucky Mick.'

I stared at Adam. 'That was very clever as well as lucky, Adam.'

'Thank you, your highness. By the way, when I'm not in such a rush I'll explain to you that rough old schools like mine also teach Latin, but never mind that right now, just call me Lucky Adam.'

Before I could reply, Bernard spoke again,

'Alors, what did you find?'

Adam leant back in the wing chair where he sat between us and stretched out his long legs. I thought how tired he looked and wondered just how much sleep he had taken over the last few days and nights, but then he sat forward again and spoke quietly,

'Pages and pages of research into micro-chipping racehorses. Not just that but old reports of stories of substitute racehorse scams in the past... long before microchips came on the scene. Then, I found a purchase invoice for a scanner and some other computer equipment purchased for cloning the microchips.'

'But surely it's not illegal to buy microchips... my own horse was microchipped, I know. Vets and trainers can all buy the chips and the equipment to implant them. I don't understand about cloning... how can that be possible?'

'I agree, but Toni said he had heard rumours about the possibility. He knows a lot about drugging and other illegal stuff and, not surprising as he has his own and Lois life savings riding on Miss Mopp, he's paranoid that they might try to nobble her. ' Adam slapped his knee in exasperation, 'But, you're so right, Princess. We still have no proof that they are up to anything illegal. There was a long list of betting websites in favourites, but I couldn't open any of them. Password wouldn't work there.' His face clouded over as he continued more slowly, 'But then there was a load of history on you, Princess. Press interviews and media links, Facebook, your own website and your publishers... loads of stuff. Then I found an email sent from Rupert to Mick five days ago. He said that he though they should call the whole thing off, as there would be increased media interest on the course because Eve Sinclair would be there.'

'So we were right about that, at least. If they don't want more cameras and reporters around than usual, then they must be up to something fishy.'

Adam was silent for a moment and then he added

'Mick's reply was there, too, still in the inbox. He said it would be best if you were stopped from showing up at the racecourse.'

'Stopped? How do they think they could do that? It's not that I really want to go, but they can't stop me.'

Bernard leaned forward, 'They can do many things... kidnap.'

I stared at Bernard and then laughed, 'Don't be ridiculous. They wouldn't kidnap me because of some stupid horse race. This is Suffolk and not exactly Mafia land.'

I spoke defiantly but my heart was racing and I found I was clenching my hands into tight fists. All through my childhood and onwards, my father had prepared me for the risk of kidnap. Even my school, full of equally wealthy girls had given lectures on the subject. Once a year a senior policeman would be called in to talk to us all. Somehow, we had all thought it ridiculous at the time. I realised that while I had been miles awy in thought, Adam had stood up,

'I have to go now to meet Toni. We're going to sleep in the stables tonight to watch over Miss Mopp. I know I can leave you, Bernard to watch over Eve as you always do.

And then he was gone. Disappeared before I could object to the idea that he should sleep in a stable... or ask if he thought a racehorse was more in need of him than I was myself.

32

I stared out into the darkness, wishing that I could suppress my feelings of impending trouble. My hotel room offered every comfort, but I shivered in the warmth. I pulled my dressing gown around me and held myself tight. Had it really been a good idea that Adam would sleep in Miss Mopp's stable? I sighed and then cleared a gap in the steamed window pane. It was raining, straight rods of rain that fell from the moonless sky and formed large puddles on the terrace below. My suite of rooms was on the third floor and had a view across to the next door stud and stables. There were security lights in the yard, but the weather was so bad that they just shimmered in the mist. I wondered if Toni's yard had similar lighting. It was a smaller establishment than this Arab-owned one next to the Royal Park. I sighed again and wondered just what I was doing in this racing world that I knew nothing about.

It had seemed a good idea to liven up my chapter on an English vineyard with finding one near Newmarket. It was all my fault that Adam was now involved with the whole mad and dangerous affair that had led him to sleep in a stable. Good idea or bad idea, there had been no changing his mind. Toni and Adam both believed that there could be an attack on Miss Mopp before the race tomorrow.

Then, I thought about Lois and doubted if she would be able to sleep either. All her life savings placed on the back of a horse. It was unthinkable. The effect of my small attempt to cheer her up with a new handbag would surely have soon worn off. I felt a rush of anger toward Toni. How could he risk their money? Bad enough to gamble with his own money but to place Lois's hard-earned money too? Even my own father had only played with his own money. But was that quite true? I knew he was accused of something to do with a pension scam, but had firmly closed my mind to understanding anything at all about the wretched matter. Maybe, one day I would devote some time to attempting to work out exactly why and what he had done to fall so spectacularly from grace.

Then, I remembered his last postcard. I hadn't had a chance to re-read it. I turned away from the window and moved quietly across the room to find my handbag. I was very aware that Bernard was sleeping, or maybe lying awake, on the sofa in the small dressing room of my suite. He had insisted on playing the bodyguard after Adam's warning, and I had not made much resistance to the idea. Now, in the low light from my bedside lamp, I took the card from my handbag and read the last enigmatic lines again. It was the first time my father had written any more than the standard "All well here, best wishes from your loving Papa." I had a little stack of these monthly cards in my desk drawer in Provence. Whenever I came across them, held neatly together with an elastic band, they were nothing more than a source of annoyance. For some reason, I could never bring myself to thrown them out. This card was becoming even more infuriating than all the rest put together. The extra line was maddening. Why couldn't my father just write like anyone else? I knew in my heart it was because he just wasn't like anyone else. He was definitely a one-off, high-flying super-brain. But, then, wasn't it likely that he had flown so high he had burnt his wings. Was he the Icarus of the City of London? Why, why had he written that extra line? I whispered the words,

"The truth may be stretched thin, but it never breaks, and it always surfaces above lies, as oil floats on water."

It was obviously a quote but not one that I knew. Not Shakespeare, I was sure of that. There was a haunting ring to the last few words. I should have known the quotation, and I felt angry again as I realised that my father expected me to recognise it. High expectations, always such high expectations. Growing up with him as my single parent, I had never known anything different. I had enjoyed his constant didactic method of upbringing. I had been a studious child and eager to meet his high standards. I suppose it had been a constant desire for his approval, although I never resented it. After his disappearance, I had determined to make my own decisions and set my own standards. I smiled at the thought as actually there hadn't been much alternative. I threw the card back into my handbag and snapped it shut, trying to hide away the frustration of not identifying the quotation.

I switched off the bedside lamp and threw myself onto the bed. I was so tired, too tired to sleep. My mind was racing as fast as any champion horse, but where was the finishing post? I smiled as I recalled Adam saying any finish would do. But how to end this business? There was still no real evidence or proof that we could pass on to the local police or Bernard's friend at the Met in London.

I got off the bed again and went over to the dressing table and turned on the little rosy pink silk shaded lamp. Now I stared into the mirror at my own dark reflection. Even in the flattering light, my eyes looked tired and ringed with shadows. I pulled my hair back from my face and peered critically at myself. I looked a wreck. stood up and quietly opened the wardrobe to flick through my new clothes that had been hung there for me. I slipped on the new high-heeled shoes and looked in the long mirror on the wardrobe door. The soft leather was comfortable, and although the heels were very high, they were expensively well-balanced. Doubtless, the grass would be sodden with the continuing rain and ruin my shoes. Miss Mopp might have big hooves but... I stopped myself from thinking about the horse, the going and, most of all, Adam sleeping on watch in her stable. Instead, I turned back toward the mirror and strutted a few steps. I looked ridiculous wearing the shoes with my kimono robe so I quickly pulled on some underwear and slipped into my new dress. Again, I turned to the mirror. Yes, better, much better. I twisted my hair up high, thinking that I might wear it knotted like Jilly's... yes, it would suit the high collar of the dress. If I were going to be kidnapped, I would at least look good.

33

I must have eventually fallen asleep, as I awoke with a start, trying to remember my dream. I closed my eyes as I struggled to get back into the scene. I had been scared, my heart was still thumping... had I been running or had I been riding a horse? Then my eyes flashed open of their own accord as I came back into a reality that was worse than my dream. I jumped out of bed and knocked on the dressing room door.

'Are you awake, Bernard?'

'*Bien sur*, Mademoiselle Eve. I am awake more than an hour. *Il est neuf heures et tout va bien*.'

'Yes, all's well. I'll take a shower and if you could order room service breakfast. I won't be long.'

'*Rien ne presse.*'

'Have you heard from Adam?'

'*Non, non... rien.*'

I turned away from the door and went into the bathroom. Nine in the morning and no news from Adam in his stable, and I had definitely not been kidnapped. How had my life managed to get into such a muddle that I need to reassure myself on those two points? I stood for a few minutes in the hot streaming water of the shower and let it wash through my hair and down over my body. If only I could let my worries and confusion go straight down the plughole. I stepped out of the shower and quickly rubbed myself dry and pulled on a robe. I could hear Bernard talking and the rattle of a trolley. I was surprised to find I was very hungry. I went through to the little living room of the suite and found Bernard examining the breakfast tray.

'Oh please, Bernard, do not tell me you are checking my breakfast. Do you think I'm going to be poisoned and then kidnapped or maybe vice versa? And as for Adam, he's spent the night sleeping with a racehorse. Whatever is it about Suffolk? Have we all gone completely mad?'

Before Bernard could reply, my mobile rang, and I rushed to answer it The small screen showed my agent's number and, as usual, I was tempted not to answer her and then succumbed to duty.

'Hi, Melanie, how are you? Not working on a Saturday, I hope? Don't you ever take a weekend off?'

I listened to her breathless, anxious voice reminding me of the lunch and the presentation and, reassuring her that I was already well aware of the event, I managed to hang up reasonably politely. I slipped the phone into my bag and turned to Bernard and the breakfast tray. Suddenly I didn't feel so hungry.

'I thought that was going to be Adam.' I wish he'd phone or at least text. Bernard poured me a coffee and added the frothy milk carefully. He passed me the cup and then, as he began to pour his own small espresso, his mobile rang. I almost dropped my cup as I jumped at the small beeping noise of an incoming text message. Bernard put down his cup and read the message on his phone with what seemed like infuriating slowness.

'Is it from Adam, Bernard, what does it say?'

Bernard looked at me, frowning, 'Is a message from Adam, yes. I read it to you. All OK at stable. Going racecourse stables with Tino + Miss M. Please bring my wash bag and decent clothes from my room. Meet at July course at 11. Tell Eve.'

Bernard and I looked at each other in silence. The Bernard's mobile rang again. This time it was the bleep of a call. I began to sip my coffee slowly, enjoying the hot strength of the caffeine. Bernard was speaking seriously, and I realised it must be Colin, his friend at the Metropolitan Police on the other end. I began to nibble on of the sugary brioches and waited as patiently as I could. After only a few minutes, Bernard ended the call and said

'That was Colin. He has decided to come to the races himself. Not on duty but he thinks there is a problem I not understand about betting but something about odds. Also he has now traced a connection between Mick Flanagan and a training yard in Ireland. He tell me more when we meet. He thinks to arrive on the course lunch time.'

'Well, it's nearly half nine now. Have some breakfast, Bernard, and then we'll put some of Adam's clothes in a bag. I guess he plans to get to the lunch we're invited to anyway. But how do we get in his room?'

Bernard smiled at me, 'I'm thinking you ask your nice friend, Mr West, to let us in Adam's room?'

'True. Yes, I 'm sure he'll understand.' I began to feel a bit better and finished off my brioche. Bernard ate a small apricot and a square of toast and then stood up.

'Now, I go to the car and check all is well. Then, I return to meet you here again. What time is good?'

'Oh, I only need half an hour or so to get ready. I suppose you're going to check the Mercedes for car bombs... usual stuff?' I laughed at the shock on Bernard's face as he followed my words and understood me.

'*Il n'y a pas de quoi rire, ça n'a rien d'amusant*, Mademoiselle Eve. Not at all funny.'

I had hoped to bring some humour into the day, but I knew Bernard was right. This whole business was no laughing matter, especially with Lois and Toni's savings running on Miss Mopp and possibly the equivalent value of another Gainsborough risked by Hugo Fellowes. No, not at all funny... even without the idea that I was not at all welcome at the races.

34

I had told Bernard that I only needed half an hour to get dressed for the races and the time was nearly up. I hated to be late, especially for Bernard who spent so much time waiting for me anyway. I looked in the long wardrobe mirror and frowned. I was ready but not happy. I had brushed my hair into a good imitation of Jilly's high topknot, but now I held my hat in my hand. How was that going to work? On my shopping spree with Lois in Cambridge, I had gone for a high level of retail therapy, on the grounds that I definitely needed it. I had spent money, not particularly wisely but with abandon. Since I had been forced to earn my own living, rather than flashing my Coutts card around with no thought of the funding behind it, yes, since then, I had certainly been rather frugal. I had a good wardrobe of classic clothes and rarely went shopping when I was in Provence. There, I could go from jeans and t-shirt to bikini and kimono without even thinking about it. The young assistant in Robert Sayle's had been more excited than I at the thought of choosing a hat for Ladies Day in Newmarket. Lois and the assistant had rushed around the millinery department bringing me one hat after another, each seeming bigger and more flamboyant than the next. Finally, as I refused one after another, I had to tell them that I didn't want to scare the horses or look like a pantomime dame. The assistant had looked disheartened and looked at Lois in despair. Then, a designer's name came to me from my wealthy past.

'I don't suppose you have anything by Philip Tracey?' The young assistant had put her hand to her mouth and looked shocked.

'Why didn't I think of that. I have three hats in a drawer from a photo shoot we did here. They're ever so special though and dreadfully... well, you know, they're to price.'

Now, I was holding one of the three hats in my hand as I looked into the mirror. It had been only a matter of moments to choose it from the other two. I knew it was for me as soon as I slipped it on my head. It was a fragile Juliet cap of flowers and leaves, skilfully woven onto an almost invisible pale ivory coloured net. It clung to the shape of my head as though it had been made for me. Or rather, it had before I had decided to yank my hair into a high bun. Now, it looked ridiculous as I tried to fit it at a jaunty angle to the left. I frowned at myself and thought how Philip Tracy would scream with horror. No, there was nothing for it but to take my hair down and leave it loose. I quickly pulled out the few hairpins and brushed my long hair as smooth as I could. Now, the hat fitted perfectly and, with the long hatpin that was hidden in one of the flower stalks, I could secure it against any Suffolk breeze that might blow across the course. I stepped into my high heels and with a nod of self-approval to my image in the mirror, I waved myself farewell and *bonne chance*.

On opening my room door, I almost fell over Bernard.

'Goodness, Bernard, you are taking this bodyguard thing seriously.' I put my hand up to my head and was pleased to find that the hatpin worked well. 'Sorry to keep you. I changed my hairstyle at the last moment.'

'Not late, Mademoiselle Eve, no problem. *Mon Dieu*, I have never seen you look more beautiful. Is very fine your new clothes... *et quel joli chapeau*!'

'Thank you, Bernard, I decided against the classic look for once. If I am to be hounded by the press all day, then I thought I'd give them plenty to write about.' I stopped as I noticed Bernard was carrying a small leather hold-all. Before I could ask about it, I saw David West strolling along the corridor toward us. He smiled, his usual welcoming smile and I had a moment to consider once again just how many professional smiles there were around, and then he spoke quietly,

'Good morning, just follow me, please.'

Then I remembered, we had to take clothes for Adam to wear, of course. I had quite forgotten in the excitement of dressing in my own new clothes. Obviously, David was about to open Adam's room for us. I felt a small quiver of excitement at the thought of seeing how Adam kept his room. Would it be as chaotic as a teenage boy's room might be? To my surprise I found that David and Bernard had stopped outside a room only a few yards along from my own. David slid the keycard into the lock and stepped aside as the door swung open. I walked in first and was immediately engulfed in the elusive perfume that was Adam. I breathed in, my senses reeling, not even trying to analyse the aroma, but missing Adam keenly. Then, I looked around and saw, to my further surprise that the room was neat and tidy to the point of minimalism. A laptop on the table under the window, a small case of different coloured USB pens. One pen, one pencil beside his small, moleskin notebook. My fingers almost reached out to pick it up, but I stopped myself. Then, I saw on the bedside table a small leather frame open with two photos. walked casually across the room until I could see it properly. One photo was a shot of me walking in a vineyard in Tuscany and the other was a close-up of my face. I turned away quickly, feeling the blood rush to my cheeks at the pleasing idea that Adam must look at me the last thing before he slept and when he awoke each morning. I noticed, too, that the leather wristband I had given him at Easter was curled up by the photos. I had bought it in Rome, at Easter, the day after he had given m a very beautiful antique silver bangle. I closed my hand over the bracelet on my wrist now and remembered the sweet moment. It was the nearest we had allowed ourselves to be a little romantic. I turned away and looked across to where Bernard was standing at the open wardrobe. This room, booked as a single room, although the bed was certainly king size, was much smaller than m suite. No small living area or dressing room, just a small shower room behind the wardrobe area. I joined Bernard the wardrobe,

'Surely his dark navy suit, Bernard? It will be a formal occasion. Can you find a white shirt? He may ever need a tie.' I turned to David who was standing waiting by the door. 'What do you think, David?'

'Well, a suit would be ideal with a white shirt, but a tie is not strictly necessary. Good shoes, though, not trainers or... er... muddy boots?' David caught my eye and I saw he was suppressing a laugh.

'Good thinking, David, you're so right. Adam will almost certainly be wearing his old muddy Timberlands.' I put my head inside the wardrobe, trying to ignore the heady perfume, at the same time as trying vainly to identify it. The strange thing was that it wasn't even like a perfume... more a breath of fresh ozone laden air, a sea breeze... but then there was the pepperminty undertone which... I realised that Bernard was talking to me.

'I find the shoes by the door. Very good shoes and very polished.'

He held out a pair of tan leather brogues that shone like conkers.

'Goodness, yes, they're fine. Of course, I remember them now. Yes, what do you think, David?'

'Ideal, handmade by Crockett and Jones if I am not mistaken. There should be a dust bag for them.'

I looked on the top shelf of the wardrobe and found a soft draw-string bag. I drew in my breath sharply as I recalled seeing similar bags hanging in my father's wardrobes. I took out the bag, uncreasing the familiar printed crest of the company with my fingers as I passed it to David. Suddenly I wanted to be out of the room,

'That's it then, isn't it? Do you have everything, Bernard?'

'Yes, I think everything, even his underclothes. *Maintenant*, now, I just I look for his wristband. The Bulgari leather band you gave him in Frascati. He asked for it most importantly.'

'I saw it on the bedside table.' I crossed the room again and picked up the bracelet and held it my hand for a moment, then passed it to Bernard. 'Anything more you can think of?' I looked from Bernard to David. The latter nodded and then said,

'Why not take a hotel towel and I notice he has his own special shaving soap in a wooden bowl... and his razor... probably his toothbrush?'

Bernard nodded in agreement, 'Already I have his wash-bag but the soap?'

I moved quickly back across the room and went into the shower room. Soap? Of course. I saw a round wooden shaving bowl lying on the basin, and I picked it up quickly, opened it and held it to my nose. I could almost feel my nostrils quivering as I breathed in the perfume. So that was it. The perfume that Adam Wright exuded, teasing my olfactory senses over the last few months... it was his own special brand of shaving soap. I gave one more sniff and then screwed the lid back on, capturing the elusive aroma. It was disconcerting, though, to find that Adam bought from the same London perfumer as my father. Of course, it was just yet another coincidence and the soap-maker was the most famous in London... as was the shoe-maker. I decided to ignore the matter and just enjoy the satisfaction of finally discovering the source of Adam's secret perfume. I passed the soap-dish to Bernard who slipped it inside the battered leather wash-bag and said,

'*On y va*, Mademoiselle Eve? Is time we go to meet Adam now.'

We left the room and David quickly pulled the door shut and smiled at us, relaxed and charming as ever.

'Well, good luck then. I may get to the races myself later.'

We walked quickly along the corridor. I was anxious now to get to the race course and find Adam.

When we reached the hotel lobby, I looked outside to the puddled gravel car park and the sodden lawns, 'I'm beginning to regret my flowery outfit. It looks more like Burberry and boots weather out there.'

We stood in the doorway for a moment looking out at the driving rain. David West moved forward, magically holding a very large umbrella,

'Your outfit is perfection, Miss Sinclair. May I congratulate you in advance on being the best-dressed lady of the day.'

'You may indeed, David, although I still think my usual trench coat look might have been more suitable.'

Bernard hurried through the rain to bring the car over to the door, and David opened his umbrella in readiness. It seemed I was back to being Mademoiselle and Miss Eve Sinclair at least for today. I sighed, thinking how I would love to hear a chirpy London voice call me Princess.

35

As Bernard swung the Mercedes into the entrance to the race course, we were immediately flagged to a halt. Bernard showed my invitation card and we were directed to the right of a long queue of cars, and to another car park. The ground was still wet although the rain had abated. The heavy car bumped slowly over the grass toward the grandstand. I checked my face in a small hand mirror that I kept in my bag. My hat was nestling rather nicely into the curve of my smooth hair and, apart from the risk of being kidnapped, I was now looking forward to the day... and to finding Adam. Another flag-bearing man signalled us to a space and before Bernard could turn off the engine, Adam appeared in front of the bonnet, smiling cheerfully. I just had time to think that it was a good job we had brought him his change of clothes, when he jumped into the car and sat next to Bernard. There was a most decided new aroma clinging to him now, the distinctive and not altogether unpleasant smell of hay and horses. He turned around to me and gave me one of his finest lop-sided grins,

'Why, Princess, you look heart-stoppingly beautiful. That dress is the very colour of your skin and is most disconcerting. And as for the hat... it must have been made by fairies just for you. It looks so beautiful... in fact, I would lay money that if it wasn't the fairies, then it's an original Philip Tracey.'

I blinked and then looked at Adam in amazement. How was it that he could always surprise me? The compliments were charming, but however did he know my hat was a Philip Tracey? But he was still talking,

'I spent a week with Philip about a year ago now, took some shots for his website. I had such a good time. It was just before I went to Afghanistan.' His handsome face suddenly looked a little older and he ran his hand over the stubble on his chin and shook his hair back as though to forget the memory. 'Anyway, I'd lay a monkey on it being a Tracey creation. Am I right?'

I remained silent as I wondered how he had coped with such a shattering difference in his lifestyle, going from the frivolous world of fashion photography to the deadly war fields. This wasn't the time to ask so I jumped to the next point,

'I think there's quite enough money being laid down on mad guesses today... still, you are right about my hat and I just hope Toni is as clever. How's Miss Mopp?'

'She's great. What a horse... I held her while Toni shoed her this morning. She's magnificent. I just hope she can race as well as Toni thinks, but she certainly has spirit.'

I looked at Adam anxiously, 'Spirit? What do you mean? Spirit, is that a good thing?'

'Well, I know nothing much about racing but she's the finest of animals. Long-legged, full of fire and yet sweetly vulnerable... she's reminds me of you, Princess.'

Before I could respond or think that this was possibly the strangest of any of Adam's compliments to me, there was a sharp rap on Bernard's window. I jumped nervously at the noise but then saw that Bernard was smiling and sliding down his window as he spoke,

'*Bonjour*, Colin, good to see you. We need to talk, yes?'

I peered curiously at the man now leaning over and talking quietly to Bernard. The rain had started to fall again, and it ran off his dark trilby and navy raincoat. He was of medium height, solidly built and almost unmistakably a policeman. Then Bernard turned to me,

'This is my friend from the Metropolitan Police, Colin Blake. Is possible that he joins us in the car to talk?'

'Of course, Bernard, *bien sur*.' I moved into the far corner of the back seat and then Adam spoke,

'No need to budge up, Princess, Colin can sit in the front. Can't have your pretty petals crushed. I'm off to shower and change. I'm betting my bag is *bien* surely in the boot, Bernard?'

Once again, before I could respond, the action moved on. The morning had an unsettling sense of urgency and pace, as though we were already heading to the winning post. I noticed Bernard give a quick brush to the front seat before Colin took Adam's place.

'Pleased to meet you, Miss Sinclair. My wife and I have watched all your programmes, this is quite an honour for me.' Colin turned around and held out hand to me.

'Thank you, pleased to meet you and thank you for all your help.'

'No trouble. I'd do anything for Bernard, he's a man in a million and has helped me before now, I can tell you... or rather I can't!'

We shook hands rather awkwardly across the back of the seat and he smiled at his own words. I nodded and wondered quite what Bernard's police career had been like. He must have taken early retirement before he began working for my father over twenty years ago. It was hard for me to imagine him as anything but my trusted friend and driver. The train of thought led inevitably to my missing father. Missing and missed. Hard as I tried to get on with my own life and carve my career there was always a niggling desire to be with him again. I thought of his postcard tucked in my bag. I had no need to look at it as I now knew the words by heart but they still remained annoyingly cryptic. I would Google them when I had a chance, but at the moment the race was the main event.

After today, I would be able to get back to London and then Provence. To complete the book was my priority. I heard my father's voice in my head, never mix business with pleasure. Well, Adam and I had agreed that so many times, but soon our shared work on this book would be over and then? Pleasure? Maybe he would come to stay with me in my place in Provence? Mid-summer, my little turquoise swimming pool... my paradise. I smiled at the idea of Adam and Eve in the garden of Eden. My sweet reverie was interrupted by Bernard's voice,

'Mademoiselle Eve. Eve! Are you ready? I drive to the entrance now.'

'Sorry, Bernard, I was miles away. Yes, of course, quite ready.'

I smoothed my hair and caught a glimpse of my own reflection in the driving mirror. Then I shrugged, gently patted my flowery hat and said to myself... ready or not, here I come.

36

From the moment I stepped out of the Mercedes, onto the damp red carpet laid over the turf, I had the distinct feeling that it would be hard work. The press were there with a vengeance, greeting me with a storm of flashing cameras and pushing microphones toward me. Colin took my elbow and gently but firmly pushed me toward the line-up of welcoming faces of officials. I switched on my celebrity smile and, ignoring any specific questions hurled at me by reporters, I managed to quietly say I was delighted to have been invited to Newmarket Ladies Day. I hastily signed a few autographs, thinking of my agent and how hard she had worked to bring me to an event like this... and secretly wondered how I could ever avoid anything like it ever again. The noise from the excited voices around me was deafening, and I could hardly hear the words of welcome from a tall man who shook my hand and then beckoned in the direction of a reception room. Colin walked close behind me as I attempted to talk to the tall man. So, had Colin now become my new bodyguard? I felt my stomach butterfly as I realised that the Metropolitan police were taking the matter seriously and I regretted that my day-dreaming had led me to miss out on the conversation between Bernard and Colin in the car.

As we moved away from the loud voices of the crowd in the entrance, the tall man, now introduced himself as Toby Mount, the chairman of the Jockey Club. Still, I smiled and nodded, wondering if I could possibly have heard his name correctly. It seemed too ideally suitable a name to fit his long, lean face and his jutting teeth. Then, to my relief, I saw Adam walking toward me, freshly showered, his long blonde hair in damp fronds around his smiling face and now elegantly dressed in his navy suit and white shirt. Thank you, Bernard and David, said to myself and went to meet him. He took my hand and kissed it then whispered in my ear.

'There's a winning shot for my paparazzi friends.' And sure enough, the flash bulbs were popping again. I was once more engulfed in his minty perfume, and I smiled properly now, my usual smile and not the fixed rictus of my earlier vacuous grin. Perhaps I could enjoy myself after all?

Soon we were seated at a long table set beside the plate glass window overlooking the race course. The rain was now lashing against the glass and pouring down the glass roof. We were in the restaurant called the Summer House, on the July racecourse, but outside it could have been early winter. I was disappointed to find that I was seated between the horse-toothed Toby on my left and, on my right, a rotund, jolly man, rosy with health or alcohol. After a few preliminary throws at conversation and the usual admiration of my wine tours on the telly, it was back to racing. I was disappointed to see that Adam was seated too far down the table to be near enough to talk to him. I watched him as the first course was served and enviously admired his easy manner. Somehow he managed to stay completely himself, jokey and casual and at the same time charming everyone in earshot. I overheard one or two men trying to draw him into talking about war, but he easily diverted them and stayed on lighter subjects. I thought how my publicity agent, Melanie, would just love to have him as a client rather than me.

I looked around the glass-roofed room, full of diners eating and drinking, mostly too much of both. There was a buzz of excitement that was definitely due to the oncoming afternoon of races. I felt another somersault in my stomach as I remembered Lois and Toni's hard-earned money all laid on Miss Mopp. Perhaps the rain would bring them luck? Then, I saw Sara and Hugo at a table in the corner with a group of friends, some of whom I recognised from the cookery school. At the same time, Sara looked up and caught my eye and held up her hand with two fingers crossed as she waved. I waved back, my heart sinking as I guessed it probably meant that Hugo had listened to Lois and placed a bet on Miss Mopp. Hugo was sitting opposite Sara, laughing and talking, possibly drinking too much, his cheeks flushed with excitement. Sara's face, even when she smiled to me, was pale and drawn and I felt a moment of sympathy for her, Lois and even the wild Miss Mopp who was oblivious to how much was riding on her back. My eyes wandered around to the door where Bernard and Colin were standing together chatting and, I assumed, trying not to look like bodyguards. They were watching the door and not looking in my direction, and I wondered if the Ferrari men hadn't even turned up. As my gaze swept back around the room, caught the merest glimpse of a grey-haired man just leaving through another exit. My heart now stopped for what seemed like several beats, and I jumped up, breathless, and ran to follow the man... for surely it was my father? I pushed my way through the small group of people at the exit and anxiously searched the crowd, but there was no-one that even vaguely resembled my father. Had it been a trick of the light, a strange illusion in my own mind? I turned back, bitterly disappointed, and found myself face to face with Bernard and Adam. Bernard spoke first, frowning as he said, almost angrily,

'*Qu'est ce tu fait,* Eve? What are you doing? Where were you going?'

I shook my head and fought back hot tears of disappointment,

'Sorry, Bernard, I was being so silly. I thought I saw my father in the crowd.'

Adam came forward in front of Bernard and put his arm around my shoulders and gave me a tight squeeze

'Oh, Princess, what a shock that must have been. I know just how that can happen. Do you want me to go an see if I can find who it was?'

I shook my head and straightened my shoulders,

'No, of course not, and how could you recognise him anyway, you've never even met him? I'm so sorry. I think I was dreaming about other things and suddenly, I just thought... anyway, of course, I was mistaken.'

'I knew your Evereveries would lead you astray one day, Princess. You are so often in your own world. Maybe you were sort of wishing he was here and...'

I interrupted him quickly, 'No, no I really wasn't. It happened out of the blue. I was just worrying about Miss Mopp winning this afternoon. Anyway, I had better get back to the table, but I wanted a chance to speak to you. Mr Mount or maybe he's Lord Mount, I'm not quite sure, but anyway... he has just asked me to present the winner of the two-thirty race with a cup. In all this noise and hubbub I could hardly make out what on earth he was on about, but I think it may be the race that Miss Mopp is in.'

Adam looked at me with his blonde eyebrows arched in surprise. 'Oh my God, Princess, yes, it is. I suppose you had to say yes. I just hope you'll be presenting it to the stable owner that Toni works for then. I haven't had a chance to tell you about the three horse bets, either?'

Now it was my turn to lift my eyebrows,

'Whatever does that mean? Honestly, this horse-racing world is another planet.'

'I can't explain now, but basically two Irish horses have been withdrawn from the race at the last moment. Something about a ferry delay shipping the horses over.'

'But that's surely a good thing, isn't it? I mean, there will be less competition for Miss Mopp.'

'It's not at simple as that, Eve.' Adam looked serious, and the way he had called my by my name and not Princess made me feel nervous. I could tell he was very worried.

'Well, at least it's still raining and isn't that what Toni said Miss Mopp liked?'

Adam didn't answer straight away, and then I saw that the main course was being served at our table and I knew it would be rude to stay talking any longer.

'We'd better go back to the table now. I don't want to be an impolite guest. I hope we can get together before the start of the race.'

Adam nodded, and we both returned to our seats. Cameras were still popping, and I sighed as I thought about what the media would make of it all the next day.

37

As coffee was served, the general excitement in the room was feverishly contagious. Some tables had already emptied, and most guests had now begun to stand by the windows. I noticed that Bernard and Colin had disappeared, and I tried to catch Adam's eye, but he was absorbed in talking to a beautiful young woman wearing a very low-cut dress. In fact, it was so low cut that there was very little material, just a bright orange satin strip, below the tattoo in her cleavage, and before it became the hem. I was pleased to see that she had rather porky legs and that Adam was actually looking over her shoulder as she shrieked with laughter. I followed the direction of his gaze and saw he was looking out the window. Then, with a brief smile and nod to the tattooed cleavage, he turned to me and stood up. I stood up, too, and we both moved toward the window and stood side by side.

'I think I should go over to the grandstand. Are you staying here to watch the race, Princess?'

'My hosts seem to have forgotten about me for the moment, they're so excited about the races. Not that I mind. I guess they'll come and find me if they want me to give away the prize or cup or whatever it is to the winner. What do you think is best? Have you seem Bernard and Colin?'

As I asked, I saw Bernard coming back into the restaurant. I waved to him, and he came over to us. He was still looking serious and he spoke quietly.

'Colin has gone down to the paddock. Rupert and Mick are there. We have been checking the tracer on the Ferrari, but they arrived in a horse box. Now, Colin has just discovered that Mick has a cousin in Ireland with a small, how you say, *établissement, écurie*... yes, training yard, you know. *Alors*, so, they have the horse called Chestnut Fire in same race as your Miss Mopp, Adam. Does your friend, Toni, know this you think?'

'He knows that two out of the three Irish horses in the race have been withdrawn not under orders.'

'This means? *Quoi*?'

Before Adam could answer, there was an increase of noise and movement, and I looked at my phone to check the time.

'Oh my God, it's nearly two-thirty. The race is about to begin. Quick!'

Bernard grasped my arm firmly and almost led me out of the restaurant. Adam followed close behind, as we walked through the throng of people and managed to find a space in the grandstand overlooking the winning post. My heart was beating fast, and I thought of Lois and how she must be suffering. Then, the commentator began to call out the jockeys colours and the horses' names as they cantered down to the starting stalls. I glanced up at the large screen which gave a close view of the scene, and realised I was looking at Miss Mopp. Adam grabbed my hand excitedly as the tall bay horse passed us at a leisurely pace, her long legs reaching out and eating up the grass. The rain had stopped, and a glimmer of sunshine glinted on her coat. She was certainly a handsome horse, and I could understand why Adam was so fond of the animal.

'She is an incredible filly, isn't she, Princess? Beautifully groomed, too. The stable girl hopes to win the best-kept horse race, too.'

'Too? You mean as well as winning the race. Please, Adam, don't wish for too much.'

He turned to look at me, his face slightly flushed with excitement, 'It never hurts to wish, Princess. I wish for so many things and do my very best to make them come true. What else is there to do?'

'I suppose you're right. Goodness, I feel so worried for Lois and Toni… and poor Sara.'

'Look, there's the Irish horse going down now. See, the chestnut, number 7 with the jock in bright blue.' Adam pointed at the screen and I saw a beautiful chestnut horse being held back by the jockey and cantering almost sideways.

'That looks a lively horse, what a beauty... but then they all look wonderful to me.' I turned to Adam and added, 'But there's so much that can go wrong. It's all luck in the end, isn't it? I just don't know how anyone can put money on a horse, not serious money like your life savings anyway.'

'I know, Toni has to be crazy and it is very unfair on Lois. I think he knows that now, but he's absolutely convinced that Miss Mopp will win. He hasn't even made the bet second past the post. Still, he did get good odds betting early on and...'

'I have no idea what you're talking about now. To me, it's just one huge risk and something I would never ever do. What was it Bernard said on our drive up here... animated roulette?'

'Yes, Bernie said that was what your father called horse-racing. Anyway, I have a good feeling about Miss Mopp pulling it off. Don't worry. Did you see that man again who looked like your Dad?'

The change of subject threw me for a moment, and I shook my head, 'No, I was just being silly. I think it may have been because I had a strange card from him. It was forwarded to me from Provence.'

'What do you mean strange? In what way.'

'Rather cryptic. It was a quotation I think. I just can't think from where.'

'Well if you don't know, my sweet little scholar, I'm sure I wouldn't. But try me... do you have it with you?'

'Oh, I remember it, "The truth may be stretched thin, but it never breaks, and it always surfaces above lies, as oil floats on water." '

'Don Quixote. It's definitely from Cervantes' Don Quixote. We did it at A level. I loved that book.'

I put my hands up to my cheeks in realisation, 'Of course, of course, it is. Don Quixote talking about honesty and truth being revealed. Yes, you're so right, Adam.' I squeezed his arm in gratitude and began to think about why my father had chosen that particular quote. I looked up at Adam, but he was concentrating on the big screen again. The horses were now nearly all in the starting stalls apart from one horse who was playing up.

Adam leant forward toward the screen, his face anxious, 'That's Miss Mopp, she doesn't want to go in the stalls. I wish I was right there with her.'

'How exactly do you calm her down, Adam?'

'No idea, I just listen to her.'

'Listen to her? I thought you had to whisper or something?'

'Hmm, maybe, I don't know, she likes to tell me what to do. Just like you, Princess. She behaves like royalty.'

I was about to object, but then I saw that Miss Mopp had finally gone into the stall and a moment later they were off. I suddenly realised that I had no idea of the length of the race.

'How long is it, Adam?'

He didn't answer, and I saw he was staring transfixed at the horses as they thundered around a bend. I looked away from the screen and strained forward to look along the race track, but there was no sign yet of the horses.

Is one-mile handicap, Mademoiselle Eve, you see on the screen, The jockey on Miss Mopp is wearing the red and white, number 3.'

I turned around and realised that Bernard was standing directly behind me, watching my back as usual and giving me the information I needed... as he had done since I was a small child. Then he added quietly,

'Your father talked many times of the Don Quixote... I think he very much liked the book and the moral, *bien sur*.' He spoke into my ear as the commentator's voice was broadcast deafeningly loud across the whole race course.

'Yes, you're right, Bernard. I'll have to think about it. It's true. Maybe he identified in a way with the chivalry and the quixotic behaviour.'

Then my words were lost in a tumult of noise, and I realised how ridiculous it was to be talking literature when the race was on. Now everyone was leaning forward and I could see a dark cluster of horses in the distance coming over a slight rise in the ground. Then, suddenly they were near, and the commentator's voice rose to a high pitch of frenzied excitement. Adam was squeezing my hand tight and shouting,

'Come on Miss Mopp, you can do it, come on my beauty.'

Then the horses were flashing past, spattering mud behind them as their hooves beat into the grass. We were well positioned at the finishing post and, to my horror, there was no doubt that Miss Mopp had come in second by at least half a length. The winning horse was most definitely the Irish horse, Chestnut Fire.

38

The shock and disappointment were simply dreadful. I felt as though I had been kicked in the stomach and I held the rail tight to stand upright as my knees buckled. Adam stood beside me, one arm around my shoulders and seemed struck dumb. Then his mobile rang. He took his arm away from me, and I thought I might even sink down to the wet grass. Bernard took my arm and said quietly,

'Come with me now, Mademoiselle Eve. The sun is hot now. Come back to the restaurant and sit down, take a glass of water perhaps?'

I did feel dizzy, and I leant on his arm gratefully, trying not to think how Lois and Sara would be feeling right now. I looked at Adam who was talking urgently into his mobile,

'Are you coming back to the restaurant, Adam. Maybe a cup of tea?'

Adam held up his hand, blocking my words and I saw his face was strained with exhaustion, but also, for some reason, he was concentrating very hard on what was being said on the phone.

'What is it, Adam? Who are you talking to?'

Again he held up his hand, now frowning at my interruption. I stayed silent and waited, it was so unlike him to be rude or even dismissive. Then he clicked off the mobile and looked at me and then Bernard,

'That was Toni. Somehow we have to insist on a steward's enquiry. He says the horse called Chestnut Fire is not the right horse? I'm going down now to the unsaddling enclosure where Toni is waiting. Eve, this is up to you. You have to call for a steward's enquiry.'

I looked at Adam in dismay and held onto the sleeve of his jacket as I could see he was about to leave me, 'Adam, whatever are you on about now? I don't really know what a steward's enquiry is... what do you mean not the right horse?'

Adam shook his head impatiently, 'Chestnut Fire is the ringer. Toni is absolutely sure that its real name is Amber Girl. He used to work at a stables in Ireland, and he is dead sure he shoed it several times. Amber Girl is a real class horse, a lookalike to Chestnut Fire but in a completely different class... it's about the weighting too... it's a handicap race. I'm going down there now to find out more. Eve, you must call for an enquiry. You simply can't give the prize to Chestnut Fire.'

My head was spinning as I tried to understand a whole new vocabulary of racing words. What he was talking about. Had we been completely wrong all week? The ringer was nothing to do with Miss Mopp but somehow a substitute with this chestnut horse? Worst of all, however could I, Eve Sinclair, only invited here as a TV personality, ever manage to call for this steward's enquiry? I didn't even know what it involved. Then, just as I was about to tell Adam that it was all beyond me, he yanked his sleeve away from my grip and ran off into the crowd. I almost stamped my high-heeled foot in annoyance and frustration. I stared down at my rain-ruined shoes and felt furious with myself and most of the rest of world. Why ever had I agreed to come to Newmarket and to be drawn so far out of my comfort zone? Behind me, I heard my name called,

'Ah, there you are, Eve. I've been looking for you. It's nearly time for the presentation.'

I turned and came face to face with Toby Mount. He was smiling broadly, and Spike Milligan's poem ran through my head 'English Teeth, English Teeth! Shining in the sun. A part of British heritage, Aye, each and every one'. Was I going mad? This was no time to be distracted with a silly verse. I straightened my shoulders and stood as tall as I could, while my brain searched like a clunky old computer for any solution to what I should do next. Then, celebrity smile reluctantly switched on, I took Toby Mount's arm.

'Sorry Toby, I was just about to go back to the Summer House restaurant to find you. What a great day now the sun has come out.'

Toby seemed pleased that I was now putting some effort into enjoying the day. I remained smiling and thought if only he knew how I really felt he would gallop a furlong away from me.

'Thank you so much for the wonderful luncheon, Toby, quite delicious. That trout was out of this world. Best I've ever eaten. You Jockey Club boys certainly know how to host a good party' The mindless words of polite society slipped easily from my lips, but my brain was still searching, searching and then... at last, I had the germ of an idea. 'Sorry, Toby, will you excuse me, that's my mobile. I'd better take it. I am supposed to be at work even though I'm having such a splendid time.'

Toby drew politely away as I took my mobile out of my bag. It hadn't rung, but I pretended to listen to a call trying to look as agitated as Adam when he was talking to Toni a few moments earlier. Then I switched off the mobile and took Toby's arm again, trying to look frightened. 'Toby, that was simply dreadful.'

He looked at me anxiously, and I tried to make my arm quiver. It wasn't too difficult to act as I was, in truth, feeling very nervous.

'Whatever is it, my dear girl. Not bad news, I hope?'

His horse face was drawn even longer, and I had a moment of guilt as I thought how I was about to lie outright to him. Then, I remembered Lois and their savings... Sara and her Gainsborough... and I took a deep breath,

'It was horrible. It was...' I shuddered dramatically. If Adam thought I looked like Greta Garbo, then I could act like her, too. 'It was a death threat. This horrid man's voice said that if I give the cup to the owner of Chestnut Fire... then... I'll be k-k-killed.'

'Good God!' Toby Mount, of whom I was becoming quite fond, put a protective fatherly arm around me and twisted his long neck around, looking from side to side, as though expecting a killer to come for me at any moment.

'I feel so frightened.' I added in a timorous voice, wondering if I was now over-acting. But Toby was now in his stride and on his mobile, talking quickly and with authority.

'Don't you worry, my dear. I shall not allow a flower on your pretty head to be ruffled. You go to the restaurant with your man, Bernard, and the race course police are sending more protection. I have called for a Steward's Enquiry.'

'You have?' I looked at Toby in amazement. How did he know that was just what I wanted? I had a foolish desire to pat him and offer him a carrot. Then, loud and clear over the sound system I heard the announcement of a steward's enquiry. A thousand or more voices gasped and a long sigh went right across the grandstands, quickly followed by an increase in loud voices and commotion.

'But I'd rather stay with you, Toby. I'd feel safer.'

I heard Bernard breathe out sharply in exasperation and I knew very well that he wanted to whisk me away in the Mercedes, away from trouble. He would have seen through my dramatic play-acting. True enough, he now spoke up,

'I think is best if Mademoiselle Eve is escorted to my car. We leave the race course.'

'Oh no, Bernard, that won't do. I'm here to give away a prize, and I'm not going to be intimidated.'

Toby looked at me in surprise at my sudden new courage.

'Attagirl! I can tell now that you're your father's daughter all right. I know your father well, you know. I'm glad to hear he's being cleared of all charges. I knew the truth would out and it would all come right for him in the end... just a lot of evil lies. Now, come along with me then. The race course police will already be down at the unsaddling enclosure, and I've phoned through to the stewards down there to keep close watch over the winner,

Chestnut Fire. Let's find out what all this jiggery-pokery is about.'

I looked at Bernard, no longer needing to act shocked. Had I missed something in the world news this week while staying in the wilds of Suffolk?

39

There was no time to think about my father as we hurried away from the rail at the edge of the race course. Toby now held my arm and swept me along, his long legs striding at a fast pace. I kept up, now resigned to my ruined shoes, walking, almost running on tiptoe to keep my heels from sticking in the wet grass. How I regretted not wearing my faithful loafers. Bernard was close behind, and I became aware that two very bulky men were walking on each side. So, Toby Mount had marshalled his foot soldiers very efficiently. It slipped through my mind that the dark-suited men could equally be my promised kidnappers, but I had to rely on Toby. As though to reassure me, at that moment, he raised a hand and both the men signalled back with thumbs' up signals. I almost laughed aloud at the whole ridiculous scene but then, remembering Lois and Sara, once again, I concentrated on the job ahead. It would have been a whole lot easier if I had any idea what to expect or knew anything at all about this bizarre racing world.

Three horse bets and ringers, microchips and cloning, scanners and scams, handicaps and weights... the words flew around in my head but made no sense. Yes, I was definitely out of my field of expertise and wallowing in uncomfortable ignorance. And what had Toby said about my father being cleared of all charges? This at least was in a language I understood, but why did I know nothing about it? I longed to ask Toby more but he was striding purposefully on, and now we were heading toward a charming thatched building that looked too pleasant to be the scene of any crime at all.

As soon as we entered, I saw Adam standing beside Toni and a look of relief crossed over his face as he came to meet me.

'Well done, Princess..' He muttered into the petals of my hat, 'You're a right royal miracle worker, my lovely, how did you manage it all? Toby Mount looks as though he's fired up to find the truth in this matter. I turned to look at Toby, and saw that Adam was not exaggerating. Toby Mount was now standing tall in the midst of a group of men, all well-dressed and looking as though they owned the race course. One of them beckoned to Toni, and he joined them, and they immediately began firing questions at him. Toni's handsome face was drawn and pale as he turned from one man to the next, looking bewildered and desperate. Then I drew in my breath sharply as I saw another smaller group of men and in the middle of that group stood the Ferrari men, Rupert and Mick. Rupert caught my eye but made no smile of recognition, more, he frowned and glared at me angrily as though this whole thing was my fault. Why and how could he think that? Bernard must have seen them at the same time, as he moved forward and blocked my view with the bulk of his broad-shouldered body.

'Mademoiselle Eve, I insist we go now, please. Leave this place now, *maintenant, s'il vous plaît.*'

I shook my head at Bernard, realising that his words, spoken in French and English, were no less than and insistent command. I hesitated then and thought how many times he had been right in the past, and I looked toward the door. Outside the sun was shining on the bright green grass and the fringed thatch edging the arched oak doorway gave the scene a tempting, almost fairylike allure. In fact, it was the real world, out there, my world where I understood what was happening. Maybe my father was out there, possibly nearby. I took one step toward the door when suddenly I was gripped by a strong arm, held in such a tight grip that the pain squeezed the air from my body. I looked at Bernard, and he was looking straight at me, his dark eyes staring in fear. Then an Irish voice spoke in my ear,

'Just do as you're told, you interfering bitch and you may get out of this alive.'

I tried to breathe, but the man, who I knew must be Mick Flanagan, was holding me so tight, one arm circling my waist, that I could feel my ribs grating together. I stared at Bernard... why was he just standing stock still... and why was Adam the same, just behind Bernard, frozen to the spot. Where were the dark-suited bodyguards when I needed them? Was I to be kidnapped now, at the very end of the game? I looked wildly around the small room, wondering why everyone was silent, transfixed, just staring at me as I began to be dragged toward the exit. Then, I felt a small jab of sharper pain in my side, just above my waist, and I knew, in an instant, that it was the barrel of a gun. I wanted to scream, but I had no breath, I kicked back with my right foot and had the small satisfaction of hearing my assailant grunt with pain as my stiletto heel made sharp contact with his shin bone. But then he dug the gun harder into the flesh between my ribs and it was my turn to cry out soundlessly, still breathless. Now, Mick was almost dragging me nearer to the door, my feet were lifted clear of the ground for a moment, and the pain in my ribs made me raise my hands to my head. Then, my fingers touched the flowers on my hat and made contact with the pearl head of the hatpin. I closed my eyes, and before I could think about it, I pulled out the pin, held it fast and with a down-swinging movement I jabbed it hard into the body of this monster of a man who was trying to abduct me. The effect was immediate, Mick released me and doubled over with pain.

I ran toward Bernard but before I could reach him, Mick had straightened up again and was now wildly swinging the gun around, pointing at me and then anyone who moved. Bernard grabbed me in his arms and swung me around so that I was behind him. Over his shoulder, I saw Adam raise his arm and there was a metallic glint as he hurled something at Mick that caught him on the side of his head. I saw the glint of dark metal as a horseshoe fell to the ground. Before Mick could recover from the shock, I saw, to my horror, that Adam was now running, his head low as though in a rugby tackle, as he faced directly into the barrel of the gun. Mick pulled the trigger, and I shrieked, my voice returning sharp and shrill. But there was no explosion, just a metallic clicking sound as Mick pulled the trigger again and again on the empty gun, before

Adam reached him and forced him to the ground. Then, there was a sudden rush of movement, and the bodyguard stood either side of Adam as he lay, pinning Mick to the floor. One of the bodyguards kicked the useless gun away from Mick's hand and, as suddenly as it had begun, it was all over.

Epilogue

My publicity agent, dear Melanie, was beside herself with glee. After several of her gushing phone calls I had almost begun to wonder if the whole terrifying affair at the race course had been some wild publicity stunt. Of course, I knew it had all been too horribly true, but there was some comfort to be had in her enthusiasm. After the Ferrari guys had been arrested by the race course police, Bernard had finally managed to get Adam and me into the Mercedes and driven away. Not that we had need of much persuasion.

Now, more than a week later, as the exaggerated whirl of publicity began to calm down, I was starting to find time to finish off the last chapter of my book. Adam had made a final selection of his photos, and we had spent several hours together, looking through them and remembering our long six-month voyage together. I found it hard to believe that we had only been together for half a year as it felt, in a clichéd way, as though I had known him forever.

I smiled as I pulled on my raincoat for it was now nearly the end of July and pelting down with rain in London. It was definitely Burberry trench coat and comfortable loafers weather today. I smiled because this was to be a very special day. Adam and I had an appointment at my, or rather our, publishers to hand over the completed manuscript for them to edit. Our work together was over. So, yes, I was smiling like the Cheshire Cat, my heart beating fast with anticipation and relief. I went into the small hall of my service apartment in Fulham and looked in the mirror. I tried for a minute to look serious, but my smile kept creeping back and I almost laughed aloud when the door bell rang. Adam was reliably on time and Bernard would be waiting outside to drive us to the publishers.

'Good Morning, Princess, you look very smiley.'
'That's just what I thought when I looked in the mirror. Isn't it great to get the final *ms* completed? Why,

you're looking very pleased with yourself, too. Same old Parka and shiny conker shoes but is that a new suit?'

'Yes, I thought I'd better brush myself up to accompany you, today.' Adam was standing in the doorway, his long blonde hair shining and almost touching the hallway light, so that a glowing halo formed around his head. I had an instant vision of him as Jesus in a painting by a Renaissance artist, Titian perhaps? Then, he shattered the dreamy image by bending down to the doormat.

'Here, you have mail.' He handed me one postcard and my stomach butterflied as I recognised the dark inky handwriting that could only belong to my father. I took the card from Adam and read it quickly,

'Oh no, he's going back.' Now, I was not smiling at all. I bit my lip in an attempt to contain my disappointment and rising anger. 'It's from my wretched, infuriating father. He says he's going back to Kerala and the new life he has made there. Then he ends with 'all my love'.' I let out a long breath of exasperation. 'As if that can mean anything when he doesn't even find time to meet me. This card was posted at Heathrow.'

Adam put an arm around my shoulder, and I let his familiar perfume calm me for a moment, as I leaned against the familiar texture of his old Parka. Then I passed Adam the card, 'Read it for yourself before I tear it up in a temper.'

Adam took the card and read it as we made our way slowly down the corridor of the apartment building.

'It's true, he doesn't say much, but I think the subtext is that he thinks it is best for you, too.'

'How on earth can you read that into it?'

'That line where he says that you have made a good life for yourself now, just as he has in Kerala.'

I snatched the card back from him and read it again and then thrust it in my handbag. I still felt angry but most of all disappointed. Then we reached the double glass doors of the vestibule, and I saw the familiar dark bonnet of Bernard's Mercedes waiting outside.

'Oh, come on then, Adam. Let's get back to enjoying the day and the good life my dear Papa thinks I have made for myself. *Bonjour, Bernard, ça va?*'

Bernard opened the back door of the car, and I slid inside, glad to be out of the rain and in the comfort of the leather seating. Adam sat beside me and I was pleased that he had chosen not to sit beside Bernard. Now, he leaned forward,

'Morning Bernie, old man. How you going?'

'*Bonjour,* Adam, young man... is enough of the old man, *merci bien.* As for going... yes, we are going to Bloomsbury, *non?*'

Adam laughed, 'Okay, sorry old boy, I meant how are you going?'

'Adam, sorry young boy, what are you talking this morning? I am going by car, *bien sur.*'

I rested my head back against the headrest and closed my eyes. It was unbelievable how, after six months of travelling together, Adam and Bernard could still make the simplest exchange of words into a whirlpool of language confusion. They carried on talking and misunderstanding each other as Adam made his usual teasing jaunts about Bernard's new girlfriend, Elaine. I was pleased to hear Bernard say that she was very well and looking forward to Bernard and his son visiting again soon. Then, I lost concentration as my head was still full of the words in my father's postcard. No confusion there, just the most annoying point-blank declaration that he was returning to India without seeing me in London. There was no other way to read it. I homed in again on Bernard's voice as I realised he was talking about Newmarket.

'...so, Colin say that is certain now that Miss Mopp is declared winner.'

I sat bolt upright in the car, 'What are you saying, Bernard? What are you talking about?'

Adam turned to me, his face alight with pleasure,

'Isn't it great, Princess. The steward's enquiry found that the microchip in Chestnut Fire had been cloned. The horse was Amber Girl, just as Toni said, and the bookies have paid out now on Miss Mopp as the winner. The Jockey Club want the whole affair hushed up as much as possible as the cloned microchip should never have got past the scanner and...'

'Never mind all that horsey stuff... are you telling me that Lois and Toni haven't lost their money after all?'

'Not just not lost... they'll have won big time. I'll call Toni later. Come to think of it... I guess Sara won't have to sell another Gainsborough either? Perhaps we should drive over to Newmarket and hear all about it?'

'Count me out, Adam. It will be a long time before I go near a race course again, Newmarket or anywhere else.'

Bernard nodded firmly, 'And I am most happy you not wanting to go back to Newmarket, Eve. How can you think it, Adam?'

'Well, Bernie, the Ferrari men won't be around, that's for sure. Colin is sorting that out. Anyway, it wasn't all bad... we had some good times there, and I could visit Miss Mopp and you, Princess, you could go and see David West and thank him for all his help.'

'I've already thanked him. I sent him a case of a rather good Saint Joseph, 2012, too. He called back to thank me and said he's off on a driving holiday in Scotland. So, you see, I absolutely do not need to return to Newmarket, thank you very much.'

Bernard nodded in agreement, '*Exactement. Mon Dieu*, Adam, so already you forget you ran at a gun pointing in your face?'

'Holy moly, Bernie, that was nothing. I had already taken the bullets out of the gun when I went through Mick's room at the hotel. How about our heroic Princess, then, with her stiletto and hat pin trickery? After her showing such guts, I was just glad I had a handy horseshoe in my pocket. Toni had given it to me as a souvenir from one of Miss Mopp's big hooves. Turned out to very useful and, although I say it myself as no-one else has, it was a mighty fine shot.'

I saw Bernard give a quick glance over his shoulder at Adam, and then he turned back to looking ahead through the windscreen, shaking his head.

'You took the bullets from the gun when you searched the room? Very clever, *bien sur*, but how did you know it was the same gun or that Mick had not loaded it again?'

'Oh, I never thought about that... anyway, I don't think Mick Flanagan's brain is the sharpest tool in the shed. I doubt he would have checked the gun... it was a dead cert, really.'

I remained silent, thinking back to that dreadful moment when Mick had pulled the trigger with the gun pointing straight at Adam's head. I shuddered and then said,

'Is there any such thing as a dead cert? Haven't I said that before on this trip? Miss Mopp may have won the race, but I would hardly call it a sure thing. Anyway, at least Lois and Toni will be able to get married and have the honeymoon they planned. I hope Sara can hold onto the winnings and invest it in the extended vineyard for their sparkling wine. Yes, I'm so glad for them all. It is great news, Bernard.'

Bernard looked into his driving mirror, and I caught him glancing at me, slightly apprehensive, 'I have other news, too, Mademoiselle Eve. News from your father.'

Now I leant forward, gripping the back of Bernard's seat, 'You've heard from my father?

'Yes, a long letter that he ask I show you if I think a good idea.'

'Why does he have to be so difficult? He's been in London, and now I'm here, why couldn't we just have met?'

'He say all in his letter. Is because he still has the court case next month and he will be back. He say that if he is seen with you now, then the media will be on his back... also take the glory... that is his word... from your new career. He say two times how very proud he is of you I show you the letter later, *non*?'

I slumped back in my seat, perplexed and yet still a little angry.

'Yes, Bernard, thank you, I think I should read it if it's all right with you. I wonder why he thought you should decide whether to show it to me or not?'

Adam turned to me, 'Oh, I think that's quite obvious. Your father didn't want to upset you, and so he trusted Bernard with the information, and thought that good old Bernie would know the best time to tell you. Hmm, I think it was a good idea. You are very emotional, Princess, and I'm sure your father didn't want to upset you

I frowned as I tried to understand Adam, but he carried on,

'I wasn't going to tell you until after we have finished at the publishers, but actually, I had a letter from your father, too.'

Once again I found myself sitting upright in shock

'You've had a letter from my father. But he doesn't even know you.'

'Well, I guess the whole world has linked us together now. I mean the media has gone way over the top this week with articles about us both. Did you read the Mail on Sunday with that two-pager about us?'

'Do you really think I would read the Mail on Sunday or any other day of the week, Adam Wright?'

I glared at Adam and then suddenly I began to laugh, and Adam threw back his head and laughed with me. There was a quiet chuckle from the driver's seat and by the time we reached the publishers we were all still laughing. The car pulled to a halt, and Bernard stepped outside, waiting for us to recover our composure. Adam rubbed his eyes and managed to speak,

'Just before we go in, Princess, I must just tell you that my letter from your Pa, apart from severely telling me that my intentions had better be honourable or else...'

'Your intentions... I hope you are joking, Adam. I think my father has rather lost his rights to ask anything about your intentions. He makes me so angry sometimes.'

'Well, I make you mad, too, now and then, Princess, but it doesn't mean anything.'

'You're so right, Adam, you do often make me mad, and you're beating right down that path now. I was in such a good mood half an hour ago. Anyway, you'd probably get on better with my father that I do... you've got so much in common.'

'Now what can you mean by that?'

'More things than you can imagine. He keeps butterscotch in his pocket, he buys his so-special shoes from the same bespoke shoe-maker... same handmade soap-maker... different perfume but just as distinctive. Then there are all the big things... the way you treat me like royalty and want to protect me from the whole world.'

I ended abruptly, suddenly exhausted by emotion. Adam was silent for a moment as though he was trying to absorb everything I had blurted out. Then he spoke very quietly,

'Do you want a butterscotch, then, Princess?'

I nodded and took the sweet he offered me and tried to smile as he continued in a brighter voice,

'Well, I can't say my grand plan was to be your father figure. Phew!' He gave a long whistle, 'But I'm glad I do have some things in common with your Dad. It will make it easier to meet him. I must say, I have been rather dreading it. He's such a big name in the world.'

'It's not very likely that you will meet him... he has just gone back to India as I told you.' I concentrated on sucking the sweet that had gone sugary in the time it had been in Adam's pocket. Still, the buttery honey flavour was most agreeable, and I did feel a little calmer. 'What else did he say in his letter, then?'

'After another long paragraph on how I'd better jolly well deserve you and never let you down... then, well, he invited us out to Kerala next week to see the eco-tourist village he's built out there.'

'What? Go to Kerala with you?'

'You don't have to make it sound such an ordeal, Princess. It's all right, he's invited Bernard, too. I looked the place up on Google and it looks idyllic... all little thatched huts, palm trees... even elephants, Princess.'

'I had thought to go straight back to Provence as soon as possible...' I found myself talking doubtfully, '... and that maybe you'd come too, Adam?'

Adam took my hand then and held it tight, his long thumb resting gently on the silver bangle he had given me in Frascati. I looked at our hands, clasped together at last and looked at the leather wristband that I had given him as a return present. It had been an exchange and a promise of love. Now, he was leaning toward me as he spoke softly,

'I'd go to the end of the world with you, my sweet Princess.' He kissed me lightly on my forehead and then put his hand in his Parka pocket, 'Here, I have another rather special butterscotch.'

I looked in surprise at the small gold foil parcel that he offered me. As soon as I held it, I knew it wasn't a sweet. I carefully unfolded the paper and then gasped with shock as I saw my ring, the very ring that I had sold at the Christies' auction. The square diamonds sparkled with a blue light as I turned it, looking at in absolute wonder.

'How did you find it? How?' Words, the substance of my life and work, now completely failed me. Adam held one finger to my lips as he said,

'Never you mind. Now then, do you know what, my most beautiful, dumbstruck Princess? It's been a great pleasure to do business with you, but now that our business is over, can we please get down to the serious business of pleasure?

I hope you have enjoyed this book and will read another from the list below. My characters flit from book to book, so don't be surprised if you find a familiar name at a dinner party or bump into someone you know in a Provençal market.

Eve, Adam and Bernard will be back as star guests in my next book…only in the pipeline at the moment with the working title 'Provençal Landscape of Love'

WINE DARK MYSTERIES

Well Chilled	Case 1: Savoie
Skin Contact	Case 2: Provence
Lingering Finish	Case 3: Roussillon
Rich Earthy Tuscany	Case 4: Tuscany
Mistaken Identities	Case 5: Frascati
A Fine Racy Wine	Case 6: Suffolk
Horizontal Tasting	Case 7: Loire Valley

ROMANTIC THRILLERS

Perfume of Provence

Provence Love Legacy

Provence Flame

Provence Starlight

Provence Snow

Dreams of Tuscany

Moonlight in Tuscany

Provençal Landscape of Love

All to be found at

www.amazon.co.uk/-/e/B00KMWZRRM

16008551R00098

Printed in Great Britain
by Amazon

"Let others quaff the racy wine,
To whom kind fortune gives the vine."

'Ode to Apollo' by Horace